EGYPT'S BLESSING

CHERISH AMORE

B.LOVE PUBLICATIONS

To my amazing husband, I love you so much, babe. We been in this thing for thirteen years, and I know so many people have counted us out, but the only thing that matters is we haven't counted us out. Our love gets stronger on a daily basis. I didn't know it was possible to love a person more than I did the day before, but baby, you changed the game for me. You're an amazing man, and everything you do for our little family is amazing. You're an even better father. Our children see you as their hero. Wherever you go, I will always follow. I love you, baby!

ACKNOWLEDGMENTS

To my Lord and Savior, I say thank you first. Without Him, I wouldn't be here today.

To my amazing mother, thank you for continuously having my back, and even reading my books, though I feel so weird, LOL!

Thank you so much B. Love. I enjoy being a part of the B.Love Publications family. I thank you for the daily knowledge you pour into me. You push me to perfect my craft.

Thank you to pen sisters and brothers. You all are amazing.

To my dear friend, Teairrah, girl, we rocking out another one. I promise when I become rich like you claim I am, insider, we going to be rich together!

To my amazing supporters, as always, thank you! I have come so far from 2013 to now, and to still have y'all rocking with me is the best feeling ever. I am thankful for each one of you.

Let's ride this wave one more time.

A NOTE FROM CHERISH

Hey, readers! We're in this thing again! Thank you for riding with me again. Whether you purchased, borrowed, or downloaded from Kindle Unlimited, I say a huge thank you.

This project I truly enjoyed writing. It was fun and raw yet very romantic. I can only hope you'll enjoy this as much as I did.

This book contains sex, explicit language, and alcohol. This story will have you in your feelings, cursing, laughing, and possible crying, but you're sure to enjoy. This is a work of fiction. though some things may resemble real life, it was not taken from anyone's life particularly. It is truly words from my imagination. I truly hope you all enjoy this work of art.

As always, my loves, happy reading!

Blessings,
Cherish Amore

One

April 2017

"Shalane, I really can't believe I let you and Will talk me into going on a blind date with this guy."

Blessing sat in her 2016 Tesla Model S, observing as patrons walked in and out of King's Arms Tavern as she spoke to her best friend Shalane on the phone. Blessing and Shalane had grown up together and had been friends since they were nine.

"What if he's psycho?"

"Girl, I know Egypt. He is *not* psycho. It's not like Will and I found some random guy off the streets to take you on a date tonight."

Blessing couldn't see Shalane's face, but she could imagine her best friend rolling her eyes to the ceiling while pursing her lips together.

"Yeah, well." She sighed heavily as she finally pressed the button near her dash to shut her engine off.

"If he's Will's best friend and I'm yours, why haven't he

and I crossed paths as much as I am at your house?" Blessing asked.

"Y'all were just never there at the same time, I guess."

Blessing imagined Shalane shrugging.

"Well, I am going in. If you don't hear from me anymore tonight, know he did something to me." Blessing giggled, but she meant every word she had spoken.

"Shut up, Blessing. Have fun and call me later. Love you." Shalane spoke the statement all in one breath and then hung up before Blessing could say a word.

Chuckling at her friend, Blessing grabbed her MCM hobo bag, then opened her car door. Her Alexander Wang heels hit the asphalt as the light, spring breeze tickled her freshly waxed legs. The breeze kissed her dimples, and it felt so good.

Blessing hit the lock button on her key fob as she sashayed her hips inside the restaurant. Inside, she adjusted her fingers on her bag. She cuffed it in her arm as she scanned the restaurant looking for the guy Shalane had described to her on multiple occasions. However, no one stood out.

"Blessing?" her name was called out in a deep yet sultry tone.

Turning around with a smile, she purred a little at his sex appeal.

"Egypt?" she mumbled, eyeing him.

"Yeah." He nodded as he held his hand out with a smile on his face.

Blessing returned the gesture, shaking his soft yet strong hands. At first glance, he took her breath away. His honey-colored skin glowed, and his round, wide eyes were the perfect shade of brown. They even housed a hint of green around the rim. His shoulder-length locs cascaded over his broad shoulders. Once he smiled, Blessing swore he was posing for a picture that would be placed in a magazine. He wore jeans and sneakers, not something Blessing was expecting for a date.

"Table's this way," he told her, leading the way.

He doesn't seem half bad. She followed him to the table, getting a better view. She was instantly attracted and oozing over how tall he was and how good he smelled.

When they reached the table, he pulled out Blessing's chair before sitting down.

He didn't hesitate to compliment her as soon as they were seated. "You're beautiful," he told her.

Blessing always received compliments. She just never saw what other people saw when she looked at her reflection in the mirror. She had silky, dark-brown skin and slanted, almond-shaped eyes. Her cheekbones were high with perfect indentions for her deep dimples. She had curly hair that hung down her back and full, heart-shaped lips while beautiful freckles accented her oval face.

"Thank you." She hadn't stopped smiling since laying eyes on him.

At first, Blessing wasn't down for the blind date, but after gazing over at Egypt and into his appealing eyes that she couldn't look away from she was happy she agreed.

This might turn out better than I expected.

"WE HAVE TOTALLY DIFFERENT VIEWS," Blessing mumbled, hoping the waiter brought the check so she could get the hell out of the restaurant.

Egypt was undeniably fine as hell, but he was far from Blessing's type. Everything was flowing up until she asked him if he believed in God. When he said no, Blessing almost cursed and hauled ass.

From the God comment, everything was downhill from there. He had a fifteen-year-old daughter, who was born when he was sixteen. He cursed a lot, where she barely said any. And what she hated most was that he was a smoker.

"What's that face for?" Egypt asked, having caught the twitch in her eyes and the curve of her lips.

"I just don't see how you can't believe in God." She sighed. "That's absurd. I think it's best I leave. Would you like for me to pay for my half?" She reached down, grabbing her bag, no longer able to wait for the waiter. She didn't even want to look at him any longer.

"What's absurd is your bougie ass already quickly finding a reason to not dig me. You a fake ass Christian," he hissed.

"What the fuck?" she spat one of the many curse words she never used. He had pissed her off.

He leaned into the table. "You heard me. 'For the same way you judge others, you will be judged, and with the measure you use, it will be measured.'"

Her mouth flew open. *Matthew 7:2. How does he even know that?* She was stunned, even embarrassed, but her pride wouldn't let her admit it.

"Fuck you," she spat angrily before standing up. She stood. "Fuck you," she repeated. "Nah, beautiful. Not tonight," he said with a wink, which pissed her off even more.

Blessing couldn't stand looking at him another second. She rolled her eyes harder than necessary before storming out of the restaurant.

"GIRL, what the hell did you do to him?" Shalane laughed into the phone. "He never wants to see you again."

Blessing sat on her bed, removing her heels, not finding

the same amusement as Shalane. Sucking her teeth, she responded, "I didn't do anything." She rolled her eyes. "The feeling is mutual. I never want to see him again either. He's fine, but that brotha is twisted."

Even if Blessing didn't want to see Egypt again, she didn't feel he had the right to feel the same way when *he* was the one in the wrong.

Shalane finally stopped laughing, turning serious.

"I'on know. I thought the two of y'all would be a perfect match. Hell, Will did too, and you know he never agrees with me. Maybe it was just timing."

"I don't care what it was. I'm good on him."

"Damn, Bless. I'm sorry."

"It's cool." Blessing quickly dismissed. "But I'll call you tomorrow after church. It's late."

Blessing attended church every Sunday. Hell, not just Sunday… every chance she could, which consisted of Tuesday prayer, Wednesday Bible study, Thursday choir practice, and anything in between. She had rededicated her life to God about eight months ago, and though she was still walking fresh in the word, she was adamant about staying faithful to it.

"Pray for me tomorrow," Shalane requested. "Love you."

"Always. Love you too."

Blessing disconnected the line. *He has the nerve to say he never wants to see me again. Tuh.* She decided to dismiss the thoughts because she wasn't about to cloud her mind with negative energy.

It was what it was, and she wasn't worrying about changing it.

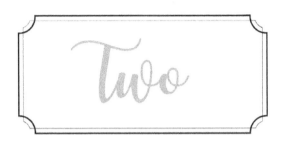

"Yo?" Egypt rolled over in his custom-built California king-sized bed, retrieving his ringing phone from the nightstand and placing it on speaker.

"I know you've seen me calling you," Martika, his annoying-ass baby's mother, echoed from the phone a lot louder than she needed to.

Egypt pinched the bridge of his nose as he sat up in the bed. "Tika, it's not even eight in the morning on one of the only two days I have off a week. How do you wake up already fired up?"

Egypt never regretted his daughter, Empress, even if he was only sixteen when she was born, but he always felt if he could rewind time, Martika wouldn't be Empress's mother. Crazy for him to feel that way when he was once madly in love with this ghetto, hot mess of a chick.

"E, I wouldn't have to call your ass if you would return my calls... or even replied to my *many* texts."

Egypt exhaled deeply, resting his against his padded headboard.

"What is it?"

Martika sucked her teeth. He imagined her with her hand on her hip, rolling her neck. "Your grown ass daughter. That's what."

Being a parent was never easy for Egypt, especially since he was forced to grow up so early when he became one. Even now, at thirty-one, he was still trying his best to be all he could. The struggle was real on a daily, not because he couldn't do it, but because Martika didn't make it easy for him.

"What she do?" He hated feeling like he was dragging the answer from her, when she was the one who had called all in an uproar.

"She is disrespectful as hell. Her grades are horrible. To be honest, I am just tired of dealing with it all."

In Martika's eyes, Empress was always a bad child, yet she never wanted to do anything about it.

Not wanting to talk to Empress through her mother, Egypt asked, "Where is her phone?"

"I got it. Her ass on punishment, and she ain't getting the shit back."

Egypt thought about it was funny that she didn't buy the phone or pay the bill but still felt she could dictate everything dealing with it.

"So you're calling me to tell me how she has been acting? I'm guessing you want me to correct her, yet you have her phone. Is that right?" He was only clarifying, but it came off more of him being a smart-ass than anything.

"E, why is it the same bullshit every time I call to tell you about *your* child?" She put an emphasis on your.

Empress was Egypt's only child, but Martika had four other younger children and three other baby fathers.

"Tika, it's not bullshit," was his reply.

Martika was horrible. But no matter how horrible she was, she was still the mother of his child. So even through all of her bullshit, Egypt never disrespected her.

"Why don't you let Empress come live with me like we talked about last time?" Egypt had a four-bedroom, three-bath home that he lived in alone, so he had an ample amount of space.

"You just want to get off child support, E," she mumbled.

Martika knew that wasn't the reason Egypt wanted Empress to live with them. Egypt was a provider no matter what. Hell, there had been times when he gave her money for the children that didn't belong to him just because she needed help.

"Keep the child support. Just let me help you out."

There was a long pause. Aside from the TV that played in the background on Egypt's end and the yelling of small children on Martika's end, there was silence.

"Fine, I'll see what she wants to do."

Egypt couldn't help but chuckle. How was it she claimed Empress was too much, yet here he was trying to help, and she really didn't want it?

"Tika, just let me know. I'm here if you need me. You know that."

"I know, E." She sighed. "Let me talk to her and think about it."

Martika's voice was the calmest it had been since she first called.

"A'ight." Soon after saying that, the pair disconnected the call.

He shook his head sliding out of bed. "Women," he said under his breath. "It's always something," he mumbled, headed to the bathroom. He knew the calls wouldn't stop from Martika about Empress, so Egypt hoped she took him up on his offer and let his daughter live with him.

Three

April 2017

B lessing pushed her buggy through Trader Joe's as she did her grocery shopping. She lived alone in a two-bedroom townhome, and since she didn't eat meat or any other animal products, she normally shopped for the meal she was having for the day.

Blessing had just picked up a bag of ghost pepper potato chips. She continued walking while reading the ingredients when she bumped her buggy into someone else's.

"I am so sorry." She apologized.

Her silky, brown-colored skin instantly took on a deep-red color as her cheeks became hot as she had looked up and saw she bumped into Egypt.

He smiled. "Why are you always apologizing?"

He was referring to how she said "sorry" at least a million times during the entire blind date before things went left that is.

There goes that smile, she thought to herself.

If it hadn't been for the mental snapshot that Blessing had taken of him before storming out of the restaurant the other night, she wouldn't have recognized him. A pair of black slacks replaced the acid-wash jeans that hung perfectly on his waist. A crisp, blue button-up shirt now replaced the plain, white T-shirt. His retro Jordans were swapped out with a pair of black dress shoes. Egypt looked the same yet so different at the same time.

"I don't know." She shrugged, never knowing it was a problem to apologize when she was wrong.

"Where'd you dip out to the other night?" He smirked.

Why does it matter? I heard you didn't want to see me again anyway.

"Um, I had to leave. I had church the next morning."

"Church couldn't wait?" He chuckled.

This mother... Blessing thought.

"No, it couldn't," she said with a smile and dimples that sank further into her cheeks.

This was the second time Blessing had seen Egypt. Each time, he was becoming less and less attractive just by the way he was acted.

"Have a good day," she politely mumbled as she pushed her buggy around him.

"Let me get your number," Egypt called after her just before she was out of sight.

Blessing wasn't one Egypt typically went after. Her brown skin was lighter than he normally preferred. Her quiet personality wasn't something he was used to. Her sandy-red, 4C natural curls were much different than the weave-wearing females he normally messed with. She was beautiful without even trying.

"Why?" She looked up at him, her head slightly tilted to the side, confused that he would want it when they were the complete opposite.

"Just hoping we can be friends."

Blessing heard the amusement in his voice, but like the few other times, she didn't see the smile on his face.

"I'm really not in the mood for anymore friends." She smiled.

Egypt didn't say a word. Instead, he continued looking at her as if he was waiting for her to change her answer. *Why would he want to be my friend anyway? We obviously have nothing in common.*

"Well, are you going to write it down or what?" she asked, shifting her weight from one leg to the other.

It was something about Egypt that had her wanting him yet hating him at the same time.

"Tell me. I won't forget it."

Blessing just knew he was playing her and was only asking for her number to see if she would give it to him. Even then, she still rambled her number off.

"I'll hit you up," he said before turning to walk away.

Blessing stood there stunned. She already disliked Egypt but wanted to love him too. He was someone she knew she had to stay away from.

———

It was crazy how Blessing said she didn't want Egypt... didn't like Egypt. Yet there she was, sitting down at her desk, on her MacBook, searching for him on Facebook.

"Dang, I don't know his last name." She sighed just as she went to Shalane's page.

She knew they were probably friends. Sure enough, they were. She clicked on his page and waited for it to load.

"Why am I like this?"

Egypt had Blessing on stalker tendency—something she

never did. Blessing hadn't even been scrolling Egypt's page a minute before her phone vibrated.

"What the?" She looked around her room, double-checking that no one was around her.

Egypt: *I want to take you on a date.*

"Who do you think you are?" she spoke to her phone.

There was no response, but she knew it was *him* because she had gotten his number from Shalane, she just never used it.

Egypt: *It's Egypt.* He sent as if he was answering her question.

Blessing: *So you did remember my number?*

Everything was telling Blessing to not bother with him. He didn't believe in God, and that was something she was big on, but even then, she couldn't stop herself.

Egypt: *I told you I would. So are you going to let me take you out on a date? Not like the blind date before. A real date.*

Blessing smiled as she continued looking at her messages

Blessing: *Sure.* She bit her bottom lip, feeling as though she was signing a deal with the devil.

Egypt: *Tonight, I will pick you up at seven.*

Blessing: *Okay.* Then something struck her.

Blessing: *Wait. How do you know where I live?* She was now nervous that he may have been spying on her.

Egypt: *I don't. I was just about to ask for your address.*

Blessing exhaled deeply, relieved to know he wasn't a stalker or some creep. After sending him her address, Blessing leaned back in her chair, smiling as she continued scrolling his page. She didn't see many pictures, but what she saw made her happy.

Tonight, on their date, she would pick his brain and get some of the answers she had been dying to know since she stormed out of the restaurant.

Four

April 2017

"R eally?" Blessing couldn't mask the fact that she was surprised about finding out that Egypt was a lead financial advisor for a local Fortune 500 company.

He chuckled. "That surprising?"

"Yeah. Umm, I mean no." Blessing quickly tried to change her answer.

Way to go judging a book by its cover, Blessing, she thought.

"I'm sorry. No offense," she added.

"None taken," he casually responded as he cut into his medium-well steak. Blessing tried her best not to turn her nose up.

Even though Egypt said no offense taken, Blessing still couldn't help but feel horrible that she didn't think he could have a good job.

"How long have you been there?"

"Going on five years."

"Oh." Again, she was shocked. This time, she played it cool as she rolled her roasted vegetable pasta around on her fork.

"What about you? What do you do?" he asked, shoving the juicy piece of meat he had cut into his mouth.

Blessing almost hurled at the sight. She never got how people ate meat. She tried not to judge though.

"I'm a physician's assistant." She beamed with pride.

Most people didn't believe her profession because of how young she was, and she could tell from the look Egypt was giving that he was one of those people.

"How old are you?" Egypt knew he should never ask a woman her age, but he knew Blessing was no more than twenty-six, if that, and for her to have the career she did, he had to know her age.

"Twenty-four." She giggled. "I graduated high school two years early. Took my college courses my senior year, getting my bachelor's. Once I was done there, I attended William & Mary without any breaks, getting my master's with honors. Then finally became a PA after attending Easter Virginia Medical School, also graduating from there with the highest honors."

"Damn, girl." Egypt sipped his drink, Looking at her.

Blessing couldn't help but smile. He enjoyed his drink, but she was socially awkward, so she hated when attention was on her.

"How old is your daughter?" she blurted out the first question that came to mind.

"Fifteen." Egypt sensed her nervousness, so he played it cool.

Fifteen? Blessing thought. If he had fifteen-year-old daughter, that meant she was born when Blessing was only nine.

"How old are you?"

Again, Blessing saw that look in his eyes where he looked as though he was smiling, yet his lips never took on that curl.

"She was born when I was really young. To be exact, I was a sixteen-year-old junior in high school," he stated, never disclosing his age.

"So you're thirty-one?" Blessing asked after quickly doing the math in her head.

"Yeah." He leaned his body back in the booth, resting his arm over the top of the seat. He'd wiped his hands and mouth with the cloth napkin before placing over top of the half-eaten steak.

"Okay..." she dragged.

Blessing agreed to come on this date to pick Egypt's brain, but she could tell he was a man of few words, who seemed to only talk when asked a question.

"So?" she dragged, placing her fork down since she hadn't taken a bite in a while anyway.

"What's up?" he replied just as the waitress came over asking if they needed anything, which they didn't.

"How long have you and Will been friends?" Again, that was the first thing that came to mind.

"Since college."

Blessing's arched eyebrow raised higher above her almond-shaped eyes. Blessing wasn't sure how he could have known Will since college when she was almost positive Will had been a dope boy his entire life.

"College?"

"Yeah. He went Howard University too—well, up until he lost his scholarship."

"Oh." Blessing never even knew he attended college, surely not a well-known school like Howard at that.

"What?' She felt uncomfortable as Egypt stared back at her.

"Let me ask you something." He sat up, tossing a wooden

toothpick into his mouth, rolling it around before settling it on one side.

"Okay."

"You never seen an educated black man, have you?"

"I have." She was embarrassed because had been passing judgment since she met Egypt.

"It's just—" She started.

"Not one that looks like me though," he said, finishing her sentence. Blessing was thinking that, but she surely wouldn't have said it.

"I'm sorry." She dropped her eyes from his piercing gaze.

Egypt couldn't help but chuckle at Blessing's closed-mindedness.

"No need to be. I just want to say society may have given you, and a lot of others, a fucked-up image of the black man, but I want to say this..." He paused while taking the tooth-pick out of his mouth. "Neither my clothes nor the way I walk or talk defines who I am as a man. Until you and the rest of this fucked-up world get that, then we will forever be thinking black men can't do shit." He leaned back again without another word, his eyes fixated on hers.

Blessing, once again, felt like shit. She wanted to apologize to Egypt and even curse all at the same time. Instead, she gave a weak smile, dropped her eyes, and looked down at the plate that she had long been done with.

The remainder of the date was more awkward than the first as they barely talked. Blessing couldn't wait for it to be over.

Five

"See? I keep telling your bougie ass. You need to stop judging folks and being so stuck-up." Shalane laughed into the phone when Blessing told her what happened when she and Egypt went on a date.

Blessing rolled her eyes to the ceiling as she exhaled much harder than necessary. People always took her being reserved with a side of shyness for being bougie or stuck up. She was also often called an old lady since she rarely drank or partied like most people her age.

"I am not bougie."

"Yeah, okay."

The line fell silent.

"What am I supposed to do?' Blessing finally asked while biting her bottom lip as she twirled one of her natural curls, something she did when she was nervous.

Blessing thought she wanted nothing to do with Egypt, but for some reason, her mind was doing its own thing.

Shalane laughed before suddenly gasping. Her girl was serious.

"Bless, are you digging him?"

"I mean…" Her worlds trailed off as she felt a vibration from her Apple Watch.

"You mean what, bitch?" Shalane knew all about Blessing dedicating her life back to God, and she respected that, but some things for her would never change. Her cursing a lot was one of them.

"Egypt just texted me." The smile she wore on her face was heard through her voice.

"Ooo, Ms. Church Girl Blessing got a thug running after her." Shalane teased.

Egypt: Hey, beautiful. Are you free? Want to grab food?

"He ain't a thug." Blessing wasn't sure why she felt the need to quickly defend Egypt, considering she had been judging him since she laid eyes on him.

Shalane cracked up laughing at Blessing defending him. Blessing sucked her teeth hard, hating to be the butt of the joke.

"Shalane, I will call you later." She sighed, knowing Shalane didn't mean any harm.

"A'ight, girl. Don't mess around and say I love you." Shalane joked before Blessing roughly pressed the red button, disconnecting the call.

Egypt: I mean, if you're busy, we don't have to. Egypt doubled texted since she didn't reply to his message.

Blessing: No, I'm not busy. We can get food.

Egypt: Bet. Can you be ready in an hour?

Blessing: I can.

Blessing: Wait. Where are we going? She didn't want to sound rude, but she didn't want to overdress or underdress.

Egypt: The beach.

Blessing: LOL! Funny.

When Egypt didn't text back, she knew the date was really at the beach.

"Oh my gosh," she whined.

Blessing was really trying to be open-minded about Egypt, but she had a feeling that no matter how open-minded she was, this wouldn't work. She hated the dirty beach water, she hated the way the sand felt between her toes, and what she hated most was Egypt didn't even ask her opinion on any of it.

———

"HEY," Blessing said, standing at her front door with a smile that slowly faded when she noticed Egypt standing at her door with two helmets in his hands.

"What's wrong?" He didn't greet her the same way she had greeted him, but he already knew what was wrong. He was asking, pretending he didn't know.

Blessing didn't want to seem like an asshole, but at the same time, she had to speak her mind.

She pointed past him to his motorcycle. "I really hope you don't expect me to get on that."

Egypt smiled, holding the helmet toward her.

"I do, and you will. Let's go."

Blessing sucked her teeth as she shifted her weight from one foot to the other while looking up at Egypt, who half smiled down at her. He never wanted to smile, but here he was now, smiling.

As much as Blessing wanted to slam her door in his face, she couldn't. As usual, it was something intriguing about him, and she had to know more.

"Fine." She surrendered. Snatching the helmet from him, she grabbed her keys from the hook and quickly slammed the door behind them.

"Don't be like that," Egypt called after her as he followed her down her walkway with a smirk on his face.

He knew he wasn't someone Blessing normally dated. Truth was, she really didn't know him well enough to know who he really was. Even though he wasn't in the business of proving anything to anyone, he felt like he had to with her.

"WHAT'S WRONG?" Egypt asked as he stepped onto the sand after slipping out of his sneakers and socks.

Blessing simply stood on the cobblestone, looking at the sand in disgust. He had brought her to Yorktown Beach, which happened to be one of his favorite places to visit to clear his mind since it was so peaceful.

"I hate the beach," she answered honestly as she scrunched her nose up. "Most people love the way the sand feels between their toes, but for me, ew, it does nothing."

Egypt watched as her nose scrunched even more.

"I'm sorry." She quickly apologized when she noticed his brown eyes observing her every move. "I don't mean to sound bougie."

"Bougie?" Egypt laughed.

"What's funny?" She didn't find the amusement he had in what she had said.

"You ain't bougie, beautiful." He didn't answer her question as he doubled back to her, kneeling in front of her with his back to her.

"What?" She was confused.

He looked over his shoulder. "Hop on and stop playing."

"What?" she asked again, though she now knew he was telling her to get on his back.

"You don't like the sand, but I do, and I am trying to

spend time with you, so get on." He continued looking back at her.

Blessing gazed deeply in his eyes as the sun reflected off them perfectly, making them seem greener. He was a perfect creation of God.

"I am not getting up until you get on."

Egypt was different. He was thuggish yet so gentle. Fine yet so rugged. Blessing wasn't looking for anything, but she could feel she had already found it.

Shrugging her shoulders, Blessing gave in and hopped on Egypt's back. He wasn't going to leave her alone until she did anyway.

Six

"It's so peaceful." Blessing was in awe as she looked out at the water while she and Egypt sat on the rocks, watching the waves crash against them.

"Indeed. This is my spot."

"What?' She peered over at him after feeling him staring at her, but he hadn't uttered a word.

"What's your story, Blessing?"

"Whachu mean?" she asked, her English horrible as she bit her bottom lip while twirling her hair. "What do you mean?" She corrected herself. Egypt chuckled.

"What is your story?" he repeated.

Blessing didn't answer. She gave a light shrug, not quite understanding his question and not wanting to answer, then it not be what he was asking.

Again, Egypt chuckled as he averted his eyes, looking out on the water before once again fixating his eyes back on her.

"You're beautiful. Probably one of the most beautiful

people I have ever laid eyes on." His voice low and deep, causing Blessing's heart to skip a beat.

Blessing knew a "but" was coming. His perfect, sexy lips were already forming it. Plus, she didn't miss it in his voice.

"But baby girl, you're shallow as fuck."

"Huh?"

He had confused Blessing. She knew a "but" was coming, but that damn sure wasn't the one she was expecting. Her mouth fell open.

Again, Egypt laughed.

"Baby, you're dope, no questions asked, but that's me basing it off of your looks, 'cause ya personality…" Once again, he paused, this time licking his lips as he leaned closer to her.

Blessing just knew he was going to kiss her. She even puckered her lips in preparation.

"Baby, let's face it. Ya personality ain't shit."

Blessing gasped.

"The fuck did you say?" Blessing quickly backed up from him, standing to her feet. He had clearly insulted her to the point that she used a forbidden curse word.

"You haven't done shit but judge me based off my clothes, the way I talk, me being a father, and even my damn locs since laying your eyes on me the first time. Yet you don't know shit about me. Let me school you real quick. I have a college degree that I received, graduating the top of my class. I am a damn good father, and I have a career where I make six figures. Yet you're still looking at my outer appearance."

"Fuck you!" she spat, quickly turning on her heels, almost falling in the process, but she didn't miss a beat as she hurried away.

Blessing was barefooted. Her pedicured toes sank down into the very sand that she hated, but she didn't care. Getting far away from Egypt was her number-one goal at the moment.

Hopping off the rock, Egypt jogged behind her, leaving his shoes as he tried to catch up with Blessing.

"Aye! Wait up." He laughed, finding amusement in the situation. He knew he would piss her off, but he wasn't expecting her to storm off.

"Leave me the hell alone!" she huffed, still using words she vowed to never say again once she was saved.

"Wait." Egypt caught up with her, grabbing her wrist. "How are you supposed to get home?" He turned her around to face him.

"Don't fucking worry about it!" She snatched her arm back.

Egypt had her cursing *and* angry—two things that were out of the ordinary for her.

"You can't walk home. It's about to be dark, and it's a long way back." The drive itself was at least thirty minutes to Williamsburg, so the walk would be hours.

"Why do you care?" She rolled her eyes hard, turning on her heels once again. Blessing didn't like the truth, and the way she blew up told it all.

Instead of following her further, Egypt stood with his feet planted, watching her hurry away. Egypt knew he had antagonized Blessing, but she had read him all wrong from day one, so he decided to give her a little piece of what she was already assuming he was like. Truth was, that wasn't him at all.

Seven

Shalane looked over at Blessing. "Egypt is on the way here," she said.

Of course, Shalane knew all about the incident at the beach. Blessing didn't miss a beat, even revealing she only made it home that evening by calling an Uber. Two weeks had passed since that date. Blessing had neither seen nor heard from Egypt since. She couldn't care less either way.

As if Egypt heard his name being mentioned, he appeared, casually walking into Shalane and Will's backyard with a much younger girl by his side.

"'Sup, Shalane," he spoke to her first once he reached them.

"Hey, Egypt," Shalane spoke as she cut her eyes to Blessing through her aviator shades, seeing if she was going to speak. She didn't.

"Hey, Empress." She looked back Egypt's way. "That is Egypt's daughter." Her eyes again landed on Blessing.

"Okay…" Blessing didn't know why Shalane felt the need to explain who Empress was.

"Hey, Auntie Sha." Empress's high-pitched voice pierced their ears as she spoke with a smile, leaning in and hugging Shalane before walking off.

"Hey, beautiful. Long time no see."

Egypt turned his attention to Blessing, who was doing her hardest not to look at him.

Blessing had her legs crossed, avoiding looking at him, but when Egypt spoke to her, she looked at him—big mistake. Egypt's eyes pierced through her soul, even though he couldn't see her eyes through the dark, tinted, oversized Michael Khors shades.

"Speak of the devil, and he shall appear." She never averted her eyes.

"So you were speaking of me?" Egypt licked his perfect lips.

Blessing didn't say a word. Not because she didn't know what to say, but she just knew the more she said, the longer Egypt would linger. She needed him gone. His cologne was hypnotizing, and his looks were worse.

"Ah, I get it." He slowly nodded his head, walking away. She clearly didn't want to be bothered.

"This nigga," Blessing mumbled, once Egypt was out of earshot.

"You're terrible," Shalane said with seriousness, which caught Blessing off guard. She would normally laugh at situations like this.

"How?"

Shalane threw her legs over the lawn chair she was reclining in, now facing Blessing.

"You do what you want, Blessing, but Egypt is legit a good dude. Keep being bougie and shit." She paused, looking over her shoulder where Egypt stood with her husband as they both looked the women's way. "Blessing, you gonna fuck around miss your own blessing that's right in front of you." Shalane stood to her feet, walking away, not giving Blessing a chance to respond.

Blessing glanced Egypt's way just as he sparked his Black & Mild cigar, instantly turning her off as she scrunched her nose.

"Yeah, okay, a good dude," she mumbled.

———

"JUST A MINUTE," Blessing called out sweetly when she heard a knock on the bathroom door as she stood at the sink, washing her hands before touching up her matte lipstick on her full lips.

No one said anything on the other end of the door, so she assumed that whoever it was walked away or was simply waiting. Smoothing over her lips, Blessing swung open the door, coming face-to-face with the guy that made the hairs on the back of neck stand up just with a smile—Egypt.

"Avoiding me?" he wasted no time asking.

"No." She sucked her teeth, hating that he knew what she had been doing.

Since Shalane made the little comment she had, Blessing couldn't help but wonder if she was right as she stole occasional glances at Egypt. It was no secret that Egypt was fine and educated. Though he didn't appear to be, from what Blessing was told, he was sweet. He just so happened to not be the typical guy she went after.

It was pure silence between the two of them. Blessing was almost sure she could hear the chatter from outside. Egypt stepped to her. For some reason, her feet wouldn't step back like her brain was telling them to.

"You want me?" he asked, his eyes fixated on hers.

"No." Blessing's breathing was sporadic.

"Tell me you don't, and mean it, and I will walk away right now and never look back."

I don't want you! Blessing was screaming in her head, but those words wouldn't leave her lips.

"I can't." Her voice came out as a whimper as she got lost in his eyes.

He stepped closer, and her breathing increased. Placing his finger under her chin, he tilted it upward before lightly stroking a stubborn curl from her face. Blessing felt like she was having an out-of-body experience. No matter what her brain was telling her to do, she couldn't follow the command. Just as Egypt smiled at her, he leaned down, kissing her lips.

Oh my gosh! His lips are so soft. Why does his tongue taste so sweet? He is not the devil, rather heaven here on earth, Blessing thought, relaxing under his touch.

The kiss was soft and sweet. Blessing wanted more. She had to have more. Closing her eyes tighter, she slipped her tongue into his mouth, allowing their tongues to dance to a tune of their own.

"Daddy?" they both heard, cutting their passionate kiss short.

Blessing was embarrassed, so much so that she stepped back from Egypt into the bathroom before slamming the door in his face.

"Um, I didn't mean to interrupt. I just needed to use the bathroom," Blessing heard Empress say from the other side of the door.

"I'll just, uh, ask Auntie Sha I if I can use the one upstairs," Empress dragged, confusion in her voice.

Egypt never said anything to Empress, but Blessing assumed she was gone when she heard a knock on the door.

"Open the door" he commanded.

Blessing wanted to ignore his knocks so badly, but like all

the other times, she was drawn to Egypt. Pushing herself from the wall that she had backed herself into, she slowly opened the door, knowing she shouldn't have but wanted nothing more than to do so.

"Stop running from me." Egypt stepped toward her while closing the door behind him with his foot.

Whether she had plans to run from him or not didn't matter anymore. He had backed her against the wall with nowhere for her go. Again, their lips touched. Blessing slowly melted like a piece of ice on a hot, summer day. She was weak for him.

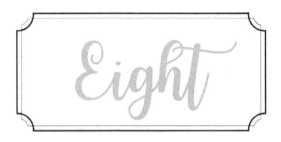

Eight

July 2017

Egypt: *Good morning, beautiful. How are you today?*

Blessing's cheeks reddened from smiling so hard. She and Egypt had gotten close over the last two months. They spent a lot of time together. With each day, she was more attracted to him. They always had deep, intellectual conversations.

Blessing: *Good morning. I am well. So glad it's Friday. How are you?*

Egypt: *You know even if I am ever having a bad day, talking to or texting you will always make it much easier.*

Blessing blushed hard. In the beginning when Egypt would say things like that, Blessing felt he was playing her or trying to butter her up for sex. But that wasn't the case, because here they were months later, and besides kissing, nothing sexual had taken place.

Egypt: *Plans for this weekend?* He double texted.

Blessing: *No. You?* Blessing already knew he would more

35

than likely be doing something with Empress as he did most weekends. Sometimes, the three of them did things together, but Blessing didn't always want to intrude on their daddy-daughter time.

Egypt: Want to come over? Empress is staying with a friend this weekend.

Blessing: Sure. Blessing was always down for hanging with Egypt. She just never showed it, because she didn't want to seem like she was suffocating him

Egypt: Don't make it seem like a task now. 😅 😂

Blessing couldn't help but laugh.

Blessing: Never that. I will see you a little later tonight.

Egypt replied with the winking emoji.

Blessing had misjudged Egypt. It was true; he was a thug at heart, but the way he handled Blessing was everything. He was a gentle giant with her.

THE CREDITS to *Moonlight* began rolling. Egypt and Blessing were snuggled close together on his bed as Blessing slept. They were supposed to be enjoying the movie together, but not long after the movie started, Blessing fell asleep. Egypt shifted his weight because it felt like he was losing the feeling in his arm. When he shifted, Blessing stirred and slowly woke up.

"The movie over?" she asked, stretching.

Egypt chuckled as she shook his arm. "Yeah. It just ended."

"I'm sorry."

"What have I told you about that?"

"I'm sor…" She bit down on her bottom lip when she realized she was about to say the word again.

"I should head out." She finally sat up, but Egypt quickly

pulled her back, so Blessing lay on her back as his body slightly rested on top of hers.

"Wha—" Her words were interrupted by Egypt kissing her lips.

"Why you tryna leave me?"

Blessing had given her life back to God eight months ago. Plus, she'd been celibate for the last four years, but along with many other things, Egypt had her wanting to throw it all away. Blessing looked up into his eyes as she reached up, lightly stroking the side of his face with her petite hand.

"It's best I do." Her voice was hoarse as she tried to convince herself.

"You wanna leave?"

"I should." She shrugged.

"But you don't want to."

Blessing shook her head.

Egypt slowly roamed her body with his massive hands, carefully tracing every inch of her like she was braille and he was blind.

"Want me to stop?" he whispered just before nestling his head between her neck and shoulder blade. He lightly kissed his way from her ear, back to her neck, before finally placing soft yet breathtaking kisses on her collarbone.

"Want me to stop?" he repeated.

Yes, she thought as she squirmed under him. "No," slipped from her full, heart-shaped lips as he softly bit her shoulder. "Don't stop," she moaned, reaching up and grabbing the back of his neck.

Egypt needed consent. Now that he had it, he had plans to take Blessing places and please her body in ways she had never experienced.

Nine

Blessing lay flat on her stomach when she woke up to the smell of breakfast cooking. Her hair was disheveled across the silk pillowcase. Rolling onto her back, she looked up at the mirrors that covered Egypt's ceiling as she bit her lip. She squeezed her thighs together, clenching the sheets between her fingers tightly, replaying last night's events over in her mind.

She so badly wanted to keep with up her celibacy, but at the same time, she wanted to fuck the shit out of Egypt. Egypt kissed her slowly before breaking it to lift her shirt over her head.

"Damn," he mumbled as he sat up on his knees peering down at her.

Blessing's body was precious, something God made. He took his time with her. Her breasts were perky, size 38Cs. She had a flat stomach, perfect waist, an ass plumped and rounded right, and thick thighs that matched.

She hated how he was gawking at her, so she shyly covered her face. No man had seen her naked in years, so she was self-conscious. Egypt couldn't help but smile down at her and her modesty. He wanted to say something about it, but instead, he kissed her flat stomach, near her navel, where a diamond butterfly piercing decorated it. She shivered under his touch.

Lifting a little, Egypt unbuttoned her jeans, slowly peeling them off her thick frame. After tossing them to the floor, he sat up, looking down at her as she lay still in her matching black lace panty and bra set. Her brown skin glistened from the moon that shined through the window.

Bending down, he kissed the top of her pelvic bone while slowly spreading her legs with his knee, leaning in and kissing the insides of both her thighs. He kissed his way down one leg and back up the other before reaching her perfectly painted, size-six, pedicured foot.

Blessing gasped as he lifted her foot, placing her toes in his mouth, slowly running his tongue over each one. Simultaneously, he reached his hands down into her panties, stroking her swollen, diamond-shaped love bud as if he was playing the strings on a harp.

"You like that?" His voice was a whisper as he ran his tongue over her big toe.

"Yeah," she moaned, biting her bottom lip.

Egypt smiled as he removed her toe from his mouth, resting it on his chest as he stopped caressing her nub to remove her panties. He peeled them off slowly as he stared deeply in her eyes. They weren't in love in the least bit and only about to have sex for the first time, but for some reason, unlike any other girl he'd had sex with, this was special, and he knew it right away.

"Hold on, baby." He stood from the bed, removing his clothes before reaching in his nightstand and pulling out a condom.

As he unwrapped the Trojan condom, he looked over at Blessing as she eyed his manhood with hunger in her eyes. Yeah, she may have been resistant and unsure at first, but now, looking at his big, *chocolate dick with veins popping out of it, she knew wanted him to take her on a ride of her life.*

Blessing's chest rose and fell quickly as Egypt positioned himself in between her legs. He kissed her while slowly piercing her flesh with the head of his dick. A faint moan slipped from her lips as she closed her eyes tightly, waiting for Egypt to fill her up quickly and the pain to stop. It hurt like a mother, but she spread her legs further, giving him full access.

"You okay?" Egypt leaned down, whispering in her ear.

"Yeah."

Egypt rocked his hips toward her.

"Mmm," she moaned as the pain she felt slowly faded into plea-sure. Reaching up, she ran her fingers through his locs as they fell over his shoulders.

Looking down, he watched her eyes closed tightly as she bit her bottom lip. That shit, along with her wet, tight center, turned him on more. Egypt sat up, tossing her legs over his shoulders, going to work.

"Stop running from this shit." He felt her hands on his rippled abs, pushing him back.

Quickly flipping her over on her stomach, he grabbed both sides of her hips, pounding her hard. He had been gentle long enough. It was time she saw what he was really about.

"Oh my God," Blessing moaned loudly, burying her face into the pillow. She seriously had to call on God in this moment; that's how good it felt.

"Egypt." She looked back at him, biting her lip hard, almost drawing blood. Her face read what are you doing to me?

At first, she was shy and covering her face, but from the way Egypt was putting it down, she was moaning, calling his name, and ready to risk it all.

"Throw that shit back." He encouraged her as she bounced her ass while he smacked it before they fell into a smooth rhythm.

Skin slapping, moans, and Egypt's shit-talking filled the room.

It was their first time having sex, but they were already addicted to the other, so it wouldn't be the last.

"I'm about to cu—" Her words were cut short as she came hard.

"Egypt..." Her moans were muffled because her face was buried deep in the pillow.

"Morning, beautiful." Egypt stepped into the room, wearing basketball shorts, carrying a tray with food on it as he interrupted her memories.

"Good morning." She bashfully sat up in the bed with a smile, running her fingers through her hair.

"We not back to this, are we?" he teased, setting the tray on the end of the bed as he walked to her.

Egypt stroked the side of her face before running his fingers through her hair, yanking lightly before kissing her deeply. Egypt was rough yet so gentle at the same time. Blessing loved how he handled her.

She blushed once the kiss broke. "No, we're not."

"Good. I didn't want to have to punish you again." He winked, referring to last night.

"Please do," she mumbled.

Egypt chuckled, not missing her comment. He wasn't one to brag, but he knew what he was doing, and he had aimed to please last night.

Blessing looked at Egypt as he slid on the bed next to her. At first, she didn't think he was her type, but now, she was second-guessing herself.

Ten

July 2017

"What does it do for you?" Blessing questioned, looking over at Egypt as he placed the cigar between his lips.

They were at his house after work, relaxing. Egypt had just ordered food, and they were in basement, which he had turned into a movie room.

"What? This?" He flicked the lighter, illuminating the dim room with the flame as he inhaled the cigar to light it.

"Yeah. Like, why do you smoke?"

"It bothers you?" he asked, ignoring her question, and instead, posing one of his own.

"It's bad for you and smells horrible," she replied in a deadpan tone.

Egypt laughed as he inhaled the cigar before slowly lifting his head, letting the smoke out of his mouth into the air.

"What's funny?" She hadn't said anything remotely funny,

yet Egypt was laughing as if she was on the stage at a comedy show.

"Nothing, baby." He chuckled.

"I won't smoke around you," he added as he sat the Black in the ashtray.

The room fell silent.

Ding dong!

Thank God, Blessing thought when she heard the doorbell ring as Egypt headed to answer it. They were waiting on food to get there that she had previously ordered.

"Baby, what you want to drink?" she heard him ask as she heard his footsteps walking back down the stairs.

"Water."

It was a Friday night. She didn't have anywhere to go. He was hoping that for one night, she would relax and have a drink, even if it was just one glass of wine.

"You sure you don't want something else?" He stood in front of the mini fridge.

"Like what?" She raised her brow.

"Wine, liquor, a shot, something." He looked back at him.

Blessing giggled. "You know I don't drink."

"I thought you did sometimes?"

"I mean, I do," she mumbled. "I do like occasionally. Not often though."

"Baby, you aren't going anywhere, so why not tonight?"

Blessing felt like he was pressuring her to drink, kind of like she was pressuring him to stop smoking. She now got why he laughed.

"I just want water," she whispered.

"Cool." Egypt nodded, grabbing the bottle of water for her and a beer for him.

She didn't want to drink, but that wouldn't stop him from doing so.

Eleven

July 2017

"Sheesh," Blessing mumbled when she was bumped for the third time in less than five minutes. She and Egypt had just come from seeing *War for the Planet of the Apes*.

"Aye, my man." Egypt's deep voice caught the attention of the obviously obnoxious, drunk man and his group of friends.

"What?" the guy turned around, slurring.

"You keep hitting my lady. Watch yourself." Egypt was calm, but Blessing knew he wasn't calm.

The guy was drunk and clearly didn't know Egypt or what he was capable of. The man looked Blessing up and down before turning his attention to Egypt.

"Fuck both of y'all!" he spat as his friends laughed.

Monday through Friday, Egypt rocked a suit, worked for a high-end company, and left his Ebonics at home, but even with all that, he couldn't hide who he was deep down from

Blessing. She was quickly moved to the side as Egypt stepped to the guy, instantly dropping him with a right hook to the jaw.

"Egypt!" Blessing yelled just as a few theater workers separated the men.

Someone, who Blessing assumed to be the manager, shouted, "Leave now, or I'm calling the cops!"

Without a word, Egypt grabbed Blessing's hand, pulling her out of the theater.

"Slow down!" Blessing yelled, pulling at Egypt's arm once they were in the parking lot.

She felt like she was being dragged. Her five-inch heels and short legs couldn't keep up with his fast stride.

"Egypt, damn!" She stopped, snatching her arm back when he didn't slow down.

"Baby, my bad." He apologized, turning to her.

She sighed, folding her arms across her chest. "Can you just take me home?"

Egypt peered at her, but she refused to look his way.

"Fuck for, baby? You were supposed to be staying at my crib," Egypt cursed, but he was calm when he spoke.

"Yeah, that was before your ass was up in there acting like an untrained thug." Blessing regretted the words the second she finished her sentence.

Egypt's jaw jumped. The way Blessing spoke to him would have gotten most people cursed out, maybe even hit, but for her, he just cut her with his eyes.

"Cool," he finally said, pushing the button on his key fob, unlocking his 2016 Maserati GranTurismo before walking to his side of the car and opening the door getting in, not even waiting for Blessing to get in.

"What the hell?" Blessing whispered.

She wanted to get home, but with the side Egypt

displayed right now, she didn't want to even get in the car with him. He didn't even open her door like he normally did.

Hearing his car being started, she finally opened the passenger door, climbing into the front seat. Blessing liked Egypt a lot, but it seemed like more and more, she was realizing the two of them weren't a great fit.

THE RIDE to Blessing's was quiet. The radio didn't even play. Blessing was okay with that. She was just ready to get out his car and get home. Egypt pulled into Blessing's neighborhood, stopping quickly in front of her house, never turning the engine off.

Blessing looked over at him. He stared straight ahead, at nothing in particular.

"Whatever," she huffed, roughly opening the door before stepping out and slamming it behind her.

Egypt pulled away from the curb without so much as a good night or making sure she made it in inside okay. Blessing wasn't expecting him to say much, but shit, after what he did, she was hoping he would at least apologize for the scene he had made.

Little did Blessing know, Egypt wasn't sorry for what he had done, and if put in the same situation again, he would react the same way all over again.

Twelve

"Has he been here?" Blessing leaned against the island in the middle of Shalane and Will's kitchen, referring to Egypt when she asked the question.

"Nah, bruh. We ain't even getting in the middle of that." Will was the one to speak, even though Blessing wasn't talking to him.

"Seriously, Will?"

It had been almost three weeks since Blessing last saw Egypt. At first, she didn't care, but she was starting to miss his good morning texts, random phone calls, date nights, pop ups, and, of course, all the forbidden sex they would have.

"No hard feelings, sis, but that shit is between you and E. Me and wifey ain't got shit to do with it," he said, putting the beer bottle he held in his hands to his lips as he walked out of the kitchen.

Blessing watched him walk away before slowly turning to look to Shalane, who simply shrugged.

"Seriously?" was all she could say to Shalane.

"Blessing, you know you my girl, but whatever you and Egypt do or don't have going on, that's something you gotta take up with him."

"Sha—"

"Bless, nah, boo. You want to talk to him or even know what's going on, call him, go by there, something. But that's between y'all, and Will and I aren't getting into it."

It pissed Blessing off that her best friend wasn't giving her the information she was prying for. She understood why, but that didn't mean she had to like it.

"Fine," she huffed, storming out of their house, pissed like a high-schooler, rather than the twenty-four-year-old woman that she was.

BLESSING FINALLY PULLED her car into Egypt's driveway. She had sat at the end of his block for thirty minutes, debating whether she should or shouldn't go to his house to talk to him. She finally said forget it and pulled up.

She noticed he had his garage door up. He was standing inside, cleaning his bike. She couldn't turn back now.

She sighed heavily, getting out of the car. "Welp, here goes nothing."

The walk from her car to the garage wasn't long, but today, it seemed like it. Even with her heels clicking against the concrete driveway, Egypt showed no interest in acknowledging her.

He didn't even look up when he said, "I was wondering how long you were going to sit at the end of the street." He had a lit Black & Mild tucked loosely between his lips as he spoke.

Wow! Blessing thought in embarrassment.

"I'm not stalking you, if that's what you think," she quickly stated.

"Never said you were." Egypt continued polishing his bike as Blessing stood there fiddling with her keys.

"Egypt?" she whispered, remembering she didn't just come over to stand and watch him wipe his bike down.

He looked up, but never stopped doing what he was doing. He inhaled the smoke from the cigar just before removing it from his lips but didn't let the smoke out immediately. His eyes pierced through her, speaking without any words leaving his lips. He slowly let the smoke escape between his lips as he waited for her to say something further. When she didn't, he looked back to his bike, doing what he was doing before she arrived.

Ugh!

"I'm sor—" She started, but quickly stopped when he looked her way. "Egypt, what do you want me to say? I was taught when I did something to hurt someone or anything remotely wrong, apologizing was the way to fix it. I'm twenty-four and have done this my entire life. Now, you want me to suddenly change?"

"Nah, I don't want you to change. I just don't understand why you're trying to change who I am though."

Blessing scrunched her face while shaking her head in confusion.

"I don't want you to change who you are. What are you talking about?"

Egypt finally stopped polishing his bike, walking to put the Black & Mild into the ashtray near where he stood before walking toward Blessing.

"You tryna change me." His tone was even, and what he was said was a statement and not a question.

"How?"

He neared her. "My smoking." He looked back at the

ashtray. "My bike, and let's not forget you just dipped on me for three weeks for what happened at the movies."

"Egypt, you broke a guy's nose. It may have even been worse if you weren't stopped."

"He fucking disrespected you, and *that* disrespect translated to me too. What did you want me to do? Let that shit slide?" he asked but didn't wait for an answer before he continued. "You digging me, but you tryna change me. I'm who you want. My image just ain't right for you. What's fucked up, though, is you don't see me complaining about you not eating meat and you turning ya nose up every time I do. Or the fact that you never take one damn drink, no matter what. Or even the fact that your ass is in church more than the damn pastor himself. I ain't changing those things about you, so stop trying to change shit about me."

"I'm not," she whispered.

"You are," he firmly said, taking a step closer to her, so their bodies now touched.

The hairs on the back of Blessing's neck stood up as she bit her lip. She wanted to reach up and twirl her hair, but there was no room between the two of them.

"I'm n—"

"Don't say it again." His voice was deep and powerful yet low and soothing.

Blessing's mouth became dry, as she looked up at him, her mouth slightly agape. She was scared and turned on at the same time.

"I'm not trying to change who you are, because even if you do shit I don't get down with, I'm feeling you, so you're free to be who you are," he spoke, leaning down, his lips touching hers with each word he spoke.

"Don't try to change me, baby, and we're good, okay?" he firmly said, pulling back.

Blessing slowly nodded her head, showing she understood. She felt his soft lips on hers again; this time, he was kissing her.

Egypt was a thug and much different than her norm, but she couldn't get enough of him, even when all the signs told her to haul ass.

Thirteen

"**H**ey, Ms. Blessing," Empress squealed, opening the front door before Blessing could even knock on it.

Empress had taken a liking to Blessing the first time she met her. It was awkward for Blessing at first because she was only twenty-four and Empress was fifteen. Not only was she young, but Blessing was afraid to get close to her because she knew there was a possibility that at any moment, things could change between her and Egypt.

"I like those shoes." Empress complimented the Tom Ford padlock black and gold open-toed heels that Blessing wore.

Blessing thought Empress was a beautiful girl. She was the girl version of Egypt, except she was one shade lighter than him. From the color of his eyes to the single mole that decorated his face near his right eye, she was his replica.

"Thank you." Blessing hugged Empress once she stepped inside.

"Where's your dad?" she asked, stepping out of the very shoes Empress had complimented.

Egypt's house was a no-shoe house. Blessing had not too long ago gotten out of church and had called Egypt multiple times, but his phone was going right to voicemail.

"His room," Empress mumbled before walking off to the game room.

Blessing sat her purse on the entryway table, grabbing her phone before she ambled up the stairs. With each step she took, her French-manicured toes sank deep into the fluffy carpet that covered his stairs. It was soft like cotton.

Before reaching the top of the stairs, Blessing heard rap music playing loudly. Without even bothering to knock, she twisted the knob, pushing the door open.

Egypt lay back on his bed with one arm behind his head and the other resting on his bare stomach, sleeping. Blessing had just gotten from church, even prayed she could resist sex with Egypt. However, even while he slept, he was her drug of choice. She needed to get high.

Unzipping the knee-length purple dress she wore, she slid both arms out of the dress before sliding it over her plump ass, letting it fall to her feet. She stood in only her red, satin panty and bra set.

Without a second thought, Blessing walked to the bed, then straddled Egypt. He instantly woke up. This wasn't who Blessing normally was, and the thought of Empress being in another room also played in her mind. It was just something about Egypt; he had her going against everything she lived for.

"Damn," he mumbled, placing his hands on the sides of Blessing's thighs, running his hands up and down them.

"I take it you missed me." He teased just as Blessing leaned down to kiss him.

Yeah, she missed him, or she was extremely horny. She

was never like this. He moved his hands from her thighs to her round, plump ass, palming both cheeks between his hands. Suddenly, there was a knock on his room door. It sounded faint since the music was so loud.

"Siri, pause the music," he said to his iHome.

"Yeah?" he answered when the music stopped..

"Daddy, Mommy is on the way here. She said I have to go home to watch my brothers and sister."

"Fuck," Egypt cursed as he tapped Blessing's thigh so she would get up. "Give me a second, Em. I'm coming out."

After stepping into a tank top and a pair of jeans she had left there, Blessing followed him out the room and downstairs. Within seconds of getting downstairs, they both heard a knock on the front door. Blessing stopped where she was and sat on the steps as Egypt snatched the door open.

"Fuck you banging on my door for?"

"I been calling you, E. Your ass ain't answering when you have my daughter over here."

Blessing couldn't see her, but she imagined her rolling her neck when she spoke.

"Tika, I was sleep, and my damn phone went dead. Also, let's not forget she my daughter too."

"Where Empress?" she asked. "Let me in, man. Hell you got me standing out here for?" Blessing heard her say just before the door was lightly pushed back and Egypt stepped out of the way.

Martika came into view and was the complete opposite of Blessing. Her skin was dark, her weave was at least thirty inches, and her body... man. She had paid good money for that.

Martika looked from Egypt to Blessing and then back to Egypt.

"Tika, Blessing. Blessing, Tika." He introduced them, closing his door behind her.

"Hey." Martika waved.

"Hey." Blessing smiled.

"So... you're the new girlfriend?" She smirked at Blessing before turning to Egypt.

"Empress told me about her. I just didn't know the infamous Egypt actually had a girlfriend." She giggled.

"Tika." Egypt's voice was calm, but his eyes showed otherwise.

"I didn't do nothing." She smirked.

"Hey, Ma." Empress interrupted.

"Let's go. Seems like your dad is too damn busy to be worried about you right now," Martika said before roughly opening the door, stepping out without another word or a second glance.

"I love you, Daddy." Empress stood on her tiptoes as he leaned down, kissing his cheek.

"I love you too, Em." He returned the gesture, watching her walk out the house.

Egypt knew Empress was sad she was leaving, but at the same time, they both were used to Martika and her ways, so they weren't surprised.

"New girlfriend?" Blessing teased with a smile once Egypt closed the door. "How many of me do you have around your daughter?"

Blessing was smiling, but at the same time, she really wanted to know if Egypt brought women around often and if she would be replaced when the next one came around.

"My daughter is fifteen, almost sixteen. Besides her mother, the only other woman she has seen me with is you."

"So you haven't been with anyone since your baby mother?" Her tone was sarcastic.

Egypt chuckled, sitting beside Blessing on the steps. "I didn't say that. I said besides her mother, you're the only other woman she has seen me with. Not the only person I have ever been with." "Oh, so you a hoe?" Blessing half joked.

Again, Egypt chuckled.

"What are you really asking?" He gently shoulder bumped her.

"Nothing." Blessing smiled a little.

She really wasn't asking him anything. Well, if he wanted to answer, she was all ears, but at the same time, she wasn't.

"She always like that?" she asked, standing from the steps.

Egypt stood with her. "Unfortunately," he replied. "Enough about her, though." He pulled her to him by the waist holding her tightly.

"About earlier?" He smiled down at her.

"What about earlier?" She flirted, biting her bottom lip.

"Don't play with me." He lifted her from her feet, palming her ass as she wrapped her legs around his waist.

They had a minor setback, but walking up the stairs with her in his arms, he had plans to pick up where they left off.

Fourteen

August 2017

Blessing stood off to the side watching Egypt interact with different people. The way he moved, talked, listened, and even stood was sexy yet powerful. He didn't have to do much, but it seemed like people flocked to him. They wanted his attention and just needed to be around him.

Egypt had been summoned to Virginia Beach for a family reunion. Of course he asked Blessing to attend. First, she declined, but then, she finally gave in. Though she was enjoying his company, she felt out of place at times. They were only an hour from home, but it seemed like a different world for Blessing.

"Ms. Blessing, are you gonna swim today?" Empress asked.

It was a good thing Empress was able to tag along with them because she helped Blessing in her shy moments.

"I am," Blessing answered, turning her attention to Empress.

No matter how hard Blessing tried, she was shy and stood back and watched others have fun, but today, she vowed to step out of her box, even if it was just to swim.

When Egypt finished his conversations, he walked to Blessing with a cup in his hand. "You good, baby?" He threw the white towel over his bare shoulder as he leaned in, kissing her cheek.

Blessing smiled. "Yeah."

"I know you don't want to go, but I came to tell you that we're about to ride jet skis."

He sipped from the red Solo cup that was half full. That wasn't her cup of tea, but for him, she was going to make it that.

"Whoa, baby! Whachu doin'?" He smiled a crooked smile as she took the cup from his hand, taking a huge gulp, barely making a face when the liquid burned her chest as it went down.

"You good?" He stared in shock as she handed him back the cup.

"We riding jet skis now?" she ignored his questions, asking one of her own.

She pushed her sunglasses on top of her head as she peered over at Egypt. He couldn't respond. He was stuck; he had never seen her like this.

"Are we going or not?"

Egypt looked at her, then to Empress, who smiled and shrugged. She hadn't seen *Ms. Blessing* like this before either.

"Yeah." He nodded slowly. He was confused, but if she was down, so was he.

"Come here, girl." He pulled her to him, never dropping his cup as he palmed her round ass that was stuffed in the jean shorts she wore.

"TWERK" by City Girls blasted throughout the campground as people drunkenly danced without a care in the world. Among those dancing was Blessing and Egypt. The shy Blessing was long gone. She was tipsy and feeling herself as she bounced and shook her ass like she as working at Magic City, trying to earn money so her lights wouldn't be disconnected.

After that one gulp from Egypt's cup, it was uphill, or downhill depending how you looked it. She had ridden jet skis, gone parasailing, played slip and slide kickball, and had drink after drink with Egypt. She was a totally different person.

"I wanna go." She turned around, facing him and running her fingers over his smooth, sculpted, bare chest. Her words barely pronounced properly like normally.

Egypt knew why she was ready go. Honestly, he was ready to go too, but he saw she was enjoying herself for the first time since meeting her, so he let it ride.

He finished what was left in his cup, reaching out for her hand so he could lead the way. "Let's go," he said.

"Em, we are going in. You have the key?" He stopped before passing Empress, who sat with her cousins.

Egypt wasn't worried about leaving Empress. She was with family. Not only that, but the way his family reunions went at the campgrounds, someone was always up and partying.

She giggled. "Yeah, Daddy. Good night. Good night, Ms. Blessing."

She could tell Blessing was drunk, and though she wasn't acting sloppy, it was funny to her since Blessing was normally all smiles and no words.

Egypt leaned in, kissing Empress before continuing to lead the way for Blessing back to the Cabin.

"DAMN, BABY," Egypt mumbled as he lay on his back in the middle of the queen-sized bed. Blessing was on her hands and knees, giving him what he named the "Blessing Super Soaker Suction 3000" head. She was the shy church girl that was letting her inner freak shine as she sucked him off, using no hands.

"Baby, you gotta stop." He felt himself about to cum. He wanted her to stop because he still wanted to slide inside her, and though she was giving him head, he was almost positive she wasn't ready to give the happy ending.

Blessing was in her zone and didn't want to stop. Not only that, but she was beyond drunk, so she was processing everything much slower than normal. It wasn't until Egypt tapped her that she moved. She flopped down, laughing as she rolled her naked body over.

"Baby, come on. I want to feel you inside of me." She tried to sound sexy, but once it reached Egypt's ears, it was nowhere near that.

Egypt chuckled as he slid the condom down over his dick before placing his knee on the bed to get on it. He didn't even have to open Blessing's legs; she was already spread eagle, welcoming her man with a full view. Egypt slid in with ease. They had been having sex so much lately that his dick had marked its territory. He was a perfect fit.

Blessing's legs wrapped around Egypt's back as they fell into a smooth rhythm. She was drunk. He was tipsy. They both had one goal in mind, which was to ride the other to their highest point of no return until either of them was ready to stop.

"Fuck," Egypt moaned.

Blessing was never boring during sex, but with her being intoxicated, it had her fucking him back while pulling him further into her, taking every inch he had to offer.

"Baby," she whimpered, clawing at his back while never slowing her motions.

She felt it, but she couldn't even say it. The buildup felt so good. Her words literally got caught in the back of her throat as she held her mouth open.

"Shit." Egypt came seconds after her as her warmth suctioned him, making it impossible for him to hold it in.

Sliding out of her, he watched as she rolled over. She pressed her thighs together just as he heard her lightly snore all before being able to dispose of the condom. He came back to the bed, laughing. Blessing had showed him a different side of her, and he was digging both.

Turning the light off, he cuddled up next to her, pulling her back to him. She never stirred as he wrapped his arms around her tightly before he joined her in sleep.

Today was a good day.

Fifteen

August 2017

"Damn, babe," Blessing heard as she continued to pretend to be sleeping. "You still sleeping? It's almost time to get back to Williamsburg."

Truth was, she was awake well before Egypt. She just couldn't bring herself to move. Opening her eyes for the first time in the morning, images of last night played in her head. She regretted everything.

It seemed fun, but that person was no longer who she was —the drinking, the wild sex, even the sexy dancing were things of the past for her. She was disappointed in herself, so much so that she couldn't even leave the bed to face Egypt.

"Baby," she heard Egypt call out as she felt his weight on the bed near her.

She couldn't pretend to be sleep forever, even if that was what she wanted to do.

"I'm getting up," she mumbled without even rolling over.

"You good, or what? You got a hangover?"

She couldn't see his face, but from the tone of his voice, she knew the smile she didn't see often was there.

"I'm fine," she told him, but the truth was that she wanted him gone.

"Well, get up." He stood, smacking her on her ass. She cringed.

Blessing hadn't lost interest in Egypt. She was disgusted that eight months of vowing to be different went down the drain in a matter of minutes.

"I'm about to go finish loading the car. When I'm done, we'll be ready." He leaned in to kiss her forehead. She wanted to die.

Blessing didn't move until she heard the door to the cabin close. Once she finally moved, she moved at the pace of an elderly lady. Flipping the light on to the bathroom, she instantly cringed, looking back at her reflection. She was still beautiful, but what she saw resembled everything but that.

Continuing to stare at her reflection, tears slowly formed.

"Lord…" Before the word slipped from her mouth, the tears had already began to fall.

She looked to the ceiling. "Forgive me. Please forgive me."

She wept. No other words left her lips as she cried hard. Blessing hated herself, but she knew God heard her cry, so that's what mattered most.

"You going to my house?" Egypt asked, backing out of the driveway after dropping Empress off at home.

The ride had been awkward and quiet. Egypt had tried talking to Blessing, but when she rarely replied to him, he turned up the music and smoked his Black & Mild—something he hadn't done around her in a while.

"No. I should go home," she mumbled. Again, he turned the music up, cruising without another word.

The ride to Blessing's only took about ten minutes, but once they reached her house, she didn't want to get out. However, she knew she had to.

"Thank you," she said, barely looking Egypt's way.

Just after opening the door, she tried to get out, but was stopped when Egypt grabbed her wrist. "What's up?" Blessing looked from her wrist to him. *Why did I do that?* she thought, automatically getting lost in his eyes.

"Egypt, you're so special to me..." She started to say before feeling his grip loosen. "But you aren't right for me."

He released her completely. Tears fell. She didn't even know they were coming. He chuckled.

"You breaking up with me?" They had never really officially said they were in a relationship, but it was obvious they were an item.

"I am not being fair to you, Egypt. We're on two different paths in life. I don't want to change you, and how I acted last night proved that given the chance, I'll change for you. I have come too far to go backwards. I'm sorry," she mumbled.

Blessing didn't want to let Egypt go, but after crying on the bathroom floor this morning, she realized they weren't equally yoked. There was no way they could mix. They were like oil and water. No matter how hard they tried, they would always be imbalanced somewhere.

For a few seconds, Egypt stared at her. Blessing was the only girl he felt could be something. She meant something to him, but he wouldn't be anyone's flunky. He slowly nodded his head. He got it.

"I'm sorry too," was the only thing he said, his eyes fixated on hers.

He didn't want to let her go, but just like her, he knew he had to, no matter how bad it may have hurt him. Blessing lingered a little. Neither wanted it to be their last time seeing the other. She knew it had to be done, and he wanted to stop her but knew she was right; he wasn't right for her.

He watched her shuffle her feet to her door, not pulling off until she was inside safely. They were done.

Sixteen

October 2017

"You look nice." Carl complimented Blessing as they walked up the walkway to Will and Shalane's house.

Carl was a guy Blessing was seeing from her church. They had only been on a handful of dates, and Blessing was already bored, but he was the type of guy she was programmed to be with. The only reason he was even with her tonight was because Shalane had come over one Sunday after church, and he was there. So when the Halloween party was mentioned, he invited himself.

Blessing had opted to go as Catwoman, which consisted of a black, thigh-length dress that looked to have been painted on and black heels. The only thing that was part of an actual costume were the ears and tail she had gotten from the party store.

"Thank you," she mumbled, walking ahead of him.

Carl was tall, sexy, educated, and he loved God. He was

basically everything Blessing needed in life. The problem was everything about him was predictable and boring. Carl was so drab. He didn't even bother dressing up for the Halloween party.

Without even knocking, Blessing turned the knob, pushing open the front door to Will and Shalane's place. They were instantly greeted by loud music, people dancing, the smell of food, and even weed smoke, which knocked the hairs in their nostrils loose.

"Bitch!" Shalane drunkenly shouted, hugging Blessing.

"Dang! Didn't the party just start?" Blessing giggled.

"So?" She laughed. "Hey, Carl," she dryly spoke. It was obvious Shalane really didn't like Carl.

"How you doing?" Carl spoke, but it didn't matter, because Shalane wasn't going to respond.

"She'll be right back." Shalane pulled Blessing away without a response from Carl.

"Shalane, what the heck?" Blessing whined as Shalane pulled her into the laundry room, closing the door behind them.

"What are you doing?" Blessing was confused.

"Egypt is on his way over here."

Blessing's heart skipped a beat but quickly returned to its normal pattern.

"So? I am with Carl." She pursed her lips together.

"What?" she asked, noticing an off look about Shalane.

"He's not alone. Vanessa is with him."

Vanessa? she thought.

"I don't care, Shalane. Again, like I said, I am with Carl." Blessing sounded believable.

"Okay, bitch." Shalane knew Blessing was lying. She saw right through her bullshit.

"Well, let's go have fun then." She snatched the door open, staggering out.

Blessing exhaled deeply. She was with Carl, and she was over Egypt, so she didn't care. Well, she did, but just like she had the last two months, she would forget him.

"Everything okay?" Carl asked once Blessing reached him. He placed his hand on the small of her back, kissing her cheek before dropping his hand.

"Yes." She gave a reassuring smile.

So many people filled the house, and smoke made it impossible to see. With the lights being dim, Blessing could only make out silhouettes of the guests. Feeling a pair of eyes glued to her, Blessing searched the room, quickly laying her eyes on the ones fixated on her—Egypt's.

Her heart skipped numerous beats, and butterflies took flight. He stood dressed in a Pharaoh's costume, and Blessing giggled inside; it was fitting. She thought she was over him, thought she didn't care, but who the hell was she fooling?

Staring at him now, he still had the same impact on her. It may have even intensified. Egypt lifted his drink, nodding his head toward her. She simply smiled and turned her attention to Carl.

Blessing could still feel his eyes on her. She wanted to avoid him, but she knew that was impossible. Before she knew it, he was walking their way.

"Oh fuck," she mumbled.

"'Sup, beautiful," he casually spoke once he reached them.

"Hey." Her mouth was dry.

It wasn't until Carl cleared his throat that she realized they were just staring at each other.

"Sorry." She looked away. "Carl, this is Egypt. Egypt, this is Carl."

Carl held his hand out. Egypt returned the gesture as he looked at him in anger.

"I'm her boyfriend." Carl must have felt intimidated.

Egypt quickly shot his eyes to Blessing. Fear consumed her.

"Boyfriend?" he was asking Blessing, but she never answered.

"Yeah." Carl pulled her to him, feeling the need to prove she was his.

Blessing was stuck. She couldn't move, nor could she speak. It wasn't until an average-looking female walked to Egypt, intertwining her arm with his and rubbing his bicep, that Blessing focused. Those were the biceps that she used to love rubbing.

Blessing's eyes narrowed as she and Egypt had a staring contest. With her eyes, she was asking who the hell was the broad.

"Baby, c'mon. Let's go smoke this Black." She held the Black & Mild between her long nails that pissed Blessing off instantly, thinking of all the bacteria she held under them.

Had she touched him with her nasty hands? Of course she had. Who wouldn't want to touch him? Had he handled her the same way he did me? Why wouldn't he when he was an expert at all he did? Did he rub her feet when they hurt like he did mine? His foot fetish wouldn't allow him not to. What about Empress? Did she know this woman?

Blessing couldn't stop her thoughts as she continued to talk to Egypt with her eyes.

"It was good see you," Egypt casually spoke to Blessing.

"Good meeting you, Carlos." He purposely said Carl's name wrong, turning walking away.

"Who is that?" Carl asked, releasing Blessing.

She couldn't answer. Her eyes were still glued to Egypt as they walked away.

"I have to use the bathroom," she mumbled, swiftly walking away after seeing Egypt lean down kissing the girl on her cheek.

BLESSING HYPERVENTILATED as she firmly pressed her hands on the beautiful marble countertop. She was over Egypt. At least she thought she was, but she knew that to be a lie as she stared back at her reflection.

"Just a minute," she huffed, hearing someone knock on the door.

Two months had passed, and nothing had changed.

"I came upstairs to use the bathroom. Why couldn't you just use the one downstairs?" she whispered from behind the door.

"I said just a minute," she said a little louder when she noticed the door being opened through the mirror.

"Why didn't I lock the door?" she mumbled while rolling her eyes when Egypt stepped in before closing and locking the door behind him.

"Who's the clown, Blessing?" he asked, folding his arms across his chest as the veins bulged from them.

"Who's the chick you brought up in here?" she fired back.

"Jealous?" His eyes twinkled but held no smile.

"Fuck you, Egypt."

"Oh, you cursing now?" He teased.

"I don't have time for this." She walked to the door as if she was going to walk through him.

"Can you move?" She avoided his eyes as she shifted her weight.

Egypt didn't say anything, and not one muscle moved.

"Don't you have a girl?" she blurted, still not looking at him.

He had gotten under her skin, and she hated it. At this point, she was ready to get out of the bathroom, find Carl, and leave. Blessing stood there, her foot tapping on the tile floor.

Silence filled the room before she finally looked his way. Her foot slowly went from a fast tap, to a slow tap, to nothing at all. She was hyped, but staring into her eyes, he calmed her.

Why does he have the effect on me?

His eyes focused on her as he watched her go from hostile to that soft relaxed Blessing he knew. That's when he made his move. Pushing from the wall, he swaddled his arms around her. Her body stiffened, but she rested her head on his chest. Their breathing patterns matched, and her body slowly warmed and melted at his touch.

He kissed her forehead just as she looked up at him, followed by her eyelids as she closed her eyes, then the tip of her nose, finally settling on her soft lips. She purred as he slipped his tongue in her mouth. They had been separated but hadn't missed beat. They memorized each other.

"We shouldn't be doing this." She pulled back, pressing her petite hand in the middle of his chiseled chest.

"But you want to?" His lips softly touched hers as he spoke.

Blessing nodded her head. She knew she shouldn't, but like chocolate, he was addiction.

Egypt kissed her again, this time lifting her from her feet and walking her to the sink. The kiss never broke as he spread her legs, pushing her dress over her butt, and snatching her panties from her body. He made quick work of pulling his pants off, along with his boxers, just as his thick, chocolate dick sprung free.

Finally breaking the kiss, he pulled her butt to the edge of the counter as he entered her sweet warmth. They gazed deeply into each other's eyes. Blessing whimpered as he filled her. She hadn't been touched since him, and her center still had the impression only he could fill.

Their lips brushed against each other's as they fell into a

smooth yet forceful rhythm. Her pussy was begging for him, and his dick fulfilled every need it longed for.

"Egypt," she moaned loudly, clasping her hands behind his neck.

"Give me that shit, baby." He encouraged her, watching her bite her bottom lip.

"I love you," he moaned.

"I love you too," she moaned loudly.

They had expressed their love for one another and didn't even realize it.

Her walls clenched him as she dripped effortlessly. She felt like a slice of heaven. They were meant for each other, but at the same time, they were horrible for each other. The saying the best sex comes from the one you aren't supposed to be with was proven to be true with them.

Blessing's moans got louder, filling the room, echoing off the walls. Egypt was punishing her center. Neither of them cared if someone heard. They were reconnecting in a way most didn't know was possible.

"Don't stop. Don't stop, baby. Please," she begged, matching his moves.

As her walls tightened, his manhood twitched. He was also at the brink. She bit her bottom lip, staring at him, sending him over the top. His cum invaded her tunnel, flowing deeply, without a drop spilling.

"Shit," he said, his tone hushed.

His dick went limp, and her legs felt heavy. Their breathing return to normal as they slowly broke eye contact, realizing what they had done.

"Umm…" Blessing frantically got down from the counter, looking down at his bare solider that was covered in her wetness.

"Oh my gosh!" She pulled her dress down over her hips.

She didn't really regret what she did, only that she did it without protection.

Egypt shrugged, casually pulling his pants up as he buckled them. What was done was already done; they couldn't change a thing. He watched her look at him one final time before storming out of the bathroom.

Egypt had seen the love in her eyes, but he knew the type of woman Blessing was. She would run from her heart just for the sake of her image. He picked up the panties that she had left behind, inhaling her sweet scent and tucking them in his pocket before leaving the bathroom.

By the time he made it downstairs, Blessing was gone, and so was her nerd of a boyfriend. There wasn't anything he could do. Blessing had, once again, already made her mind up.

November 2017

It was a repeat for Blessing as she woke up with last night's images in her head. The difference between today and two months ago was that she wasn't drunk, and she didn't feel horrible. She woke up craving Egypt. The way he kissed her last night caused her to tuck her lips tightly. His hands roaming her body made her feel the most protected ever.

She craved him; she needed him. She kept telling herself they couldn't be together, and she knew what was right for her. However, at the same time, she was a junkie, and he was the only thing that satisfied her craving. She had to have what wasn't good for her.

"Good morning," she heard, and without popping her eyes open, she sighed as last night played in her head again.

"Blessing, slow down," Carl called out as she dashed out of the house. She was of few words when she told him that she was leaving.

He caught up with her. "What happened? Why are you ready to go?"

"Carl, I just want to go home," she mumbled.

"Is it because of that guy?"

Blessing stopped abruptly. There was so much she wanted to say.

"Don't speak on something you know nothing about."

"But is everything okay?" Carl asked, reaching out and touching her arm.

"Can you just take me home please?" She continued walking.

Carl wanted answers. However, this was the first time he had seen her so upset, so he didn't utter another word.

The ride was quiet to Blessing's place, and once Carl pulled into her driveway was the first he spoke. "Want me to come in?"

"No." Her answer was flat as she climbed out of the car. There was no kiss, goodbye, or anything.

He watched her walk into her house without with even looking back. After pondering for a few seconds, he finally backed out of her driveway.

This night was nothing like Blessing expected it to be. At this point, she wanted to shower, get in bed, and try again tomorrow.

She hadn't even removed her heels when her doorbell chimed.

"Carl, just go home," she mumbled, walking to answer the door.

She knew it was him since she barely acknowledged him as she got out of his car. He was probably back to say something like, "God laid it on my heart not to end this night this way, blah blah."

"What?" She snatched her door open.

"E-Egypt?" she stuttered.

"What are you doing here?" she asked but really didn't care. Inwardly, she was happy he was there.

Egypt didn't answer the question or make a peep as he took a step toward her, causing her to back up. His eyes never left hers as he closed the door with his foot.

"What are you doing here?" Her breathing was shallow as Egypt stepped closer to her, backing her into the wall near her front door.

Again, no words left his lips as he gently grabbed her neck before kissing her. His eyes never closed, but he watched hers close. She wasn't his, but he knew she belonged to him. He wanted her.

After Blessing had left the party, Egypt said his goodbyes, even leaving Vanessa at the party, rushing to Blessing's place. He waited down the street for her to come home, and once he saw Carl leave, he made his move. He had to have her.

"Egypt?" Her voice was barely a whisper as she studied his eyes after the kiss broke.

"Don't run from me, Blessing." His voice vibrated her.

Blessing bit her bottom lip. She felt like she had the devil and an angel on her shoulder, both battling for her to pick them.

"Don't run," he repeated.

"Okay." She slowly nodded.

Egypt lifted her from her feet, carrying her to her room where he fucked her slowly and passionately. They had expressed their love earlier. Though neither of them repeated it again, the way they touched each other and brought the other to their climax while staring into each other's eyes, the love was evident.

"Good morning." She finally rolled over with a smile, looking over at Egypt.

He sat fully clothed with his back to her. He kissed her deeply as he leaned toward her.

"I've gotta go. Call you later?" He stood from the bed.

Blessing sat up. The satin sheets wrapped around her naked body as she watched him closely.

"Yeah," she mumbled.

Last night was fun. The sex in the bathroom at Will and Shalane's and the all-night sex they had in her bed was good, but even then, she knew they couldn't be an item.

Before leaving out, he kissed her forehead, and she blushed. Hearing the door close, she plopped back on her bed, staring at the ceiling. Her life had been a whirlwind lately. Though she was still confused, she knew what she was feeling was amazing, even if it might not last long.

November 2017

"Yeah, I'll call you later." Blessing squirmed from Egypt's grip as nibbled on her neck while she talked on the phone with Carl.

She and Egypt had been having sex on the regular lately. Blessing hated herself for cheating on Carl, but they weren't having sex, and she couldn't rid herself of Egypt, even when she tried.

"Why are you always playing?" She faced Egypt after disconnecting the call.

"Whacha talkin' 'bout?" He played dumb.

Blessing sucked her teeth while rolling her eyes.

"Whatever," she mumbled, stepping out of his grasp. "Today is your birthday. That is what we should be focused on."

It was Egypt's thirty-second birthday, but for him, it was just any other day.

"So?" He stepped to her, but Blessing stepped back, turning her back to him.

"Hang on. Let me send Carl this text."

Egypt took a step back.

"How long we gon' do this, Blessing?'

She faced him, raising her brow.

"Do what, Egypt?"

"This. Us. You and Carl. How long we gon' be sneaking around playing and shit?"

When they had sex back in October, it was unexpected, but now, whenever they were around each other, sex was expected. Egypt was cool with that. What he wasn't okay with was them fucking like it was going out of style, yet she was with Carl in the streets.

"I don't know." She nervously giggled as she shrugged, biting her lip as she twirled her hair.

"This side-dude shit, or whatever you think I am, is getting real old," he admitted. "This shit ain't what I'm down with."

She shrugged. She wasn't expecting this. She thought Egypt enjoyed this like she did, but obviously she was thinking wrong.

"Fuck we doin' here?"

"Having sex."

"That's it?"

"Ummm…" Her words trailed off. "Yeah, Egypt. I'm with Carl. You know that. Not only that, but you're with Vanessa."

"Vanessa don't mean shit to me, Blessing. You know that."

She shrugged.

"It's cool for us to fuck and shit, but being in a relationship is out of the question?" he sneered. "When you and I was kicking it, you always felt bad after we had sex, but now, that's all your ass is using me for."

She didn't have any words since what he said was technically right. And now, here she was, in a relationship with someone else, unable to get enough of Egypt.

"You don't even like dude, but since his clown ass into church and shit, that's who you with."

"Egypt, w—" She wanted to plead her case.

"Nah, fuck that, Blessing. Tell me right now, me or him."

"Don't do this." She reached over to him, but he stepped out of her reach.

"Which one, Blessing?" he questioned firmly. "You gon' be with my thugged-out ass, whose dick you love. Or you choosin' the flunky?"

Blessing was stuck. Truth be told, she wanted Egypt, but nothing had changed, and as before, she didn't want to change him.

"Please." She batted her thick lashes.

"Pick!" His voice was thunderous.

Blessing exhaled, staring into his beautiful eyes and looking over his beautiful face. Egypt possessed it all, all except the love for God that Blessing needed in a man.

"I'm sorry," she whispered, dropping her head.

"Fuck," he mumbled.

He knew she wouldn't pick him, but he was halfway hoping she would. She wouldn't make eye contact with him as he stared at her. He finally spoke again.

"Get out," were his last words to her before leaving his own house.

Blessing's head stayed down as tears flowed from her eyes before finally dropping on her shoes. She hated this. She hated life, but this was how it was supposed to be, even if she didn't want it this way.

December 2017

"Can I have everyone's attention?" Shalane stood with Will by her side as she held up the champagne glass in her hand.

"Will and I would like to thank everyone for joining us for our first annual Christmas dinner. Y'all know he and I love having gatherings here at the house. If you're here, that means we value you as family. That, or you came with some someone that we value as family." She cut her eyes to Blessing, who sat beside Carl, and then to Egypt, who sat beside Vanessa. Neither Carl nor Vanessa were family; they were only there by default.

Blessing hadn't seen Egypt since the day she told him she couldn't be with him. She and Carl had walked in Shalane and Will's house holding hands, looking as though they were madly in love. Spotting Egypt tonight, the feeling she always got when she saw him quickly ambushed her body as she felt caught, releasing Carl's hand quickly.

Egypt had looked up, feeling her presence. When their eyes connected, he looked away as if he didn't know who she was. It hurt, but she understood it. She had dismissed her true feelings for a guy she clearly didn't even like.

"Again, we thank you all for coming. Enjoy yourself." Shalane finished.

Carl cleared his throat.

"May I?" he asked, looking to both Shalane and Will.

Shalane waved her hand, rolling her eyes, irritated that he had spoken. Her hand wave was indication to proceed.

Blessing sat, waiting to see what the hell was so important that he had to stop the dinner party.

"I have to do this now before I chicken out."

Blessing tuned him out. It wasn't until he grabbed her hand, pulling her to her feet just before dropping to one knee, that she gasped.

"What the fuck?" Egypt sat up, looking on.

Blessing stood, looking around at everyone. She was nervous and wasn't expecting this. *Why would he propose?* They hadn't even been dating long. Hadn't even said I love you. Hell, they had barely kissed. So why would he propose?

He pulled the ring out just as he asked her to be his wife.

Her mouth went dry. She was confused, stuck, and surprised. She hadn't even given him an answer when he slipped the ring on her finger. Bad move.

Anger filled Egypt as he jumped across the long, formal table, knocking Carl off his feet. Patrons began screaming as Blessing was knocked to the ground from the impact.

Egypt didn't stop at knocking him over. He was landing punch after punch as blood began to spew. Carl fought back, but he was no match to the trained beast that was Egypt. The screams continued as some tried to break the fight up while others dodged the crossfire.

"Egypt!" Blessing screamed, standing and trying to get Egypt to stop hitting Carl. She got elbowed in the process.

Not long after the fight started, a loud banging was heard at the door right before it burst open. The Williamsburg Police swarmed the room. A small commotion took place before Egypt was safely placed in handcuffs as a police officer rendered aid to Carl.

"Sorry." Blessing apologized just as Egypt was walked out of the house, headed to jail.

Egypt's eyes were on her, but he looked as though he was looking through her. He didn't even acknowledge her apology before he was led outside.

Blessing looked around as people frantically left. Carl sat, getting his wounds nursed, and Will and Shalane both stared at her in disappointment.

Blessing may not have told Carl to propose, but the game she had been playing led them to this point. Like a puppy that had just been punished, Blessing hung her head, shuffling her feet, and walked out of the house. She had to right her wrong, and fast.

Twenty

December 2017

Blessing sat on the cold, steel chair with her legs crossed, bouncing her Nike-covered foot. The building was cold, unwelcoming, and the last place Blessing wanted to be, but she had to do it.

"Blessing Jones?" she heard her name being called and didn't move right away. It wasn't until it was called again that she stood.

"That's me." She walked to the small, bulletproof window.

"Egypt DeSean Roberts does have a bail," the oversized woman stated, popping her gum as she clacked her long, red nails on the keyboard much louder than she needed to.

"How much is it?" Blessing drawled when she never stated a price.

The lady tapped a few more keys as she continued popping the gum like it was going out of style. She didn't even look up.

"His bail is set at ten thousand dollars."

Sheesh! Blessing thought.

"Only ten percent is due to get him out of jail."

Thank God.

"So you wanna pay it or not?" She finally averted her eyes from the screen, peering over at Blessing.

"Yeah." Blessing dug in her crossbody, pulling out her wallet and retrieving her credit card.

She passed the card to the clerk. "How long will it take for him to be released?"

"I'on know." She swiped Blessing's card, tearing off the receipt. "Sign these." She slid some papers to Blessing.

She quickly read and signed them before sliding them back.

"Someone will call you up when he is being released. Until then, you can have a seat." She slid Blessing's card and receipt back to her.

Blessing had just paid one thousand dollars to bail Egypt out. Considering this mess was hers, she would have paid the full ten thousand to right her wrong.

Blessing stuffed her things back in her purse, then went to sit down as instructed by the unprofessional lady. Once again, she was back in her seat, waiting for Egypt to be released.

———

Two hours had passed, and Blessing's name had finally been called, so now she sat waiting again. This time, it was for Egypt. She knew Egypt and was pretty damn comfortable with him, but waiting for him right now had her nervous, more nervous than she had ever been in her life.

The loud sound of a door unlocking caused Blessing to look in that direction. The door slowly opened, and Egypt stepped out. It had only been about nine hours since he was arrested, but seeing him, the butterflies that always appeared swarmed crazily in her stomach.

Smoothing over the Chapstick she had applied earlier, Blessing stood, meeting him halfway. Egypt hugged her tightly before releasing her. Blessing felt the hug. It was tight, but something was off about it.

"You good to leave?" she mumbled.

"Yeah, I am."

He grabbed her hand as they both walked out of the jail.

———

BLESSING PULLED in Egypt's driveway. They had been quiet the ride there. It was weird, but they had finally made it to their destination.

"Eg—" She started, placing the car in park, but he cut her off.

"Let me talk, Blessing." His voice was calm.

He peered at her before his eyes landing on her left hand that was still decorated with the ring that Carl had proposed with. He pinched the bridge of his nose.

"Blessing, I appreciate you bailing me out, but after this, I'm good on you."

What he said caused Blessing to gasp.

"You kept saying we couldn't be together because I was a thug or I was the one that was fucked up." He chuckled. "Everything fucked up that has happened with us has been because of you." He pointed at her. "So yeah, I may have a past of being a thug, but that ain't who I am anymore, but you… your ass a bougie thug that plays victim when shit gets real." Again, he chuckled.

Blessing sat shocked. Her feelings were hurt, but she didn't say word.

"Gone 'head and marry dude that's up to speed for you,

but stay the fuck away from me. We had fun when we were together, but that shit is dead. You won't see me at any event you attend for Will and Shalane again. If for whatever reason you do, look the other fucking way. I'ma pay you back first thing Monday morning for bailing me out. I appreciate it. We done though, Blessing." Those were the last words he spoke before climbing out of Blessing's car and closing the door behind him. He didn't look back.

Tears fell the second the door closed. Although she was done with Egypt, she still held a piece of him. And after hearing his words, she knew there was no chance of them being together.

Finally leaving his house, she drove further away, her vision blurred, knowing they were officially over.

January 2018

Blessing sat at work, leaning on her desk, biting her bottom lip while twirling her hair as her leg bounced out of her control. So much had changed in the last month. Of course she and Egypt were done, but so was she and Carl. She didn't love him, and no matter how much he was her programmed guy, she couldn't do that for the rest of her life.

"What does it say?" She looked up at Shalane.

Shalane dropped back in the chair that sat in front of Blessing's desk.

She stared at the pregnancy test that Blessing had gotten from the supply office.

"Bitch, you're pregnant."

"Oh my gosh." Blessing ran her fingers through her hair as she dropped her head, looking at the other two pregnancy tests that also confirmed her pregnancy.

She only took the tests because she was two months late.

She just didn't pay attention to it until she missed this month.

"Bitch, what are you going to do?"

Blessing quickly looked up.

"You cannot tell Egypt," she quickly mumbled, realizing that was what Shalane was asking her.

"Blessing, y—"

"I said don't, Shalane," Blessing stated firmly.

Shalane stared at her.

"Fine," she said, finally giving in.

"He has the right to know." She stood. "Call me when you get off. Love you."

With that, she waved, walked out of Blessing's office, and closed the door behind her.

"Holy fuck," Blessing mumbled. She couldn't help but stare at the positive pregnancy test that lay before her.

Blessing knew she had gotten pregnant at Will and Shalane's Halloween party since that was the only time she and Egypt had unprotected sex. She was almost twenty-five, and here she was, pregnant by a man that didn't want anything to do with her.

"God, help me," she whispered, knowing what she needed to do but unsure of how to do it.

She hoped God would show her the way.

THE DAY HAD DRAGGED for Blessing. When five o'clock rolled around, she hauled ass out of her doctor's office, rushing to the one place she knew was safe—her parents' house.

"You have to tell him, Sweat Pea," her father said, holding her as she cried.

Blessing was the youngest of four. Her parents were much older as she was born when her mother as going through the change of life. Her parents were in their mid-sixties, and besides their age, they weren't old.

"Daddy," Blessing whined.

"He's right, darling." Her mother stroked her curly hair.

"You're pregnant by that man. He has the right to know. That is not something you can keep from him," she added.

Blessing heard them both loud and clear, but telling Egypt wasn't something she was ready to face just yet. Yeah, she was pregnant with his baby, but how could she face him after him telling her he wanted nothing to do with her?

"Ugh." She sighed.

Her parents could have asked questions like why she had unprotected sex, or even why she was having premarital sex, but neither of them did.

"You don't have to tell him today, but Blessing, we raised you correctly, so you know, no matter how bad you may not want to, he has to know." Her father lifted her face so that her eyes met his. Wiping her tears, he kissed his daughter's forehead.

"It's not the end of the world, Sweet Pea." He smiled, and she returned the gesture.

He said it wasn't the end of the world, but to her, it felt like it was. Shalane told her, her parents told her, she even knew she should tell Egypt, but even with all of that, she still had no plans of telling him a thing.

Twenty-Two

As usual, Blessing was at Shalane and Will's for a get-together. No matter the occasion or time of day, they were always having something. Blessing loved it since she didn't have to cook or clean up after.

This was the second gathering at Shalane's where she had managed to not see Egypt, and she was grateful because she wasn't sure how she would be able to handle that.

Blessing was making her plate, casually talking to one of Shalane's aunts when she heard a familiar voice. She didn't even have to turn around to know it was Egypt. Her heart had sped up, and the butterflies took flight. Her back was to him, and she refused to turn around.

Egypt spoke to everyone when he walked into the room— well, everyone except Blessing. She smelled him. He was close.

"Lemme talk to you," she heard to the left of her. When

no one responded, she looked to see Egypt, standing closely to her, looking at her.

"Me?" she asked, already knowing the answer, confused as to why he wanted to talk to her after all these months.

"Yeah." He tilted his head, telling her to come on.

"I'm kind of busy." Blessing didn't want to talk to him. It was already taking strength for her not to look at him. So she knew that if she walked away with him, she might become weak.

"I gotta ask you something."

Blessing looked around the room as everyone stared at them.

She turned to look to him. "You can ask me right here."

Egypt looked down at her, almost as if he didn't want to ask his question, but she said he could, so he said fuck it.

"You pregnant?" The second it rolled off his tongue, the room fell completely silent.

Oh my God. Shalane had told him.

"Um… I… um," she stuttered.

"Yes or no, Blessing?"

"Yeah, Egypt," she mumbled, shifting her weight from one foot to the other.

"Is it mine?"

Her eyes narrowed. He had offended the fuck out of her.

She laughed. "Seriously?"

"As a motherfucker."

There was neither a smile on his face nor amusement in his voice. He was dead ass.

Blessing set the plate down, then faced him. This was a private moment, but it wasn't so private anymore as everyone watched them like they were watching the biggest game of the century.

"Egypt, you know who the fuck I am."

He chuckled when she cursed.

"You know damn well I haven't fucked anyone else."

Egypt wanted to play? Well, she had time today, so she would play too.

Again, he laughed.

"I'on know, Ms. Sunday's Best. I thought you were a woman of God, but here you are cursing and shit, something you claimed you never did. Not to mention you were about to marry that bitch ass nigga."

The more he spoke, the more her eyes narrowed.

"I mean, why wouldn't you fuck someone you're about to marry? 'Cause shit, I was clapping them fucking cheeks on a fucking daily, and we damn sure weren't going to get married."

This motherfucker here.

"Fuck you, Egypt!" she hissed.

"Already did that, baby. I'm just here trying to see if I'm that kid's father." He pointed to her stomach. "Or does it belong to someone else your ass played holier than thou with?"

Blessing snickered, running her tongue slowly over her perfect teeth. She got what it was. She slowly nodded.

"You know what? It doesn't even matter, man. Suddenly, I just sleep with anyone, so nah. It ain't yours." She sounded hurt as her eyes lingered on his a little longer before storming off.

Egypt knew he should have run after her—hell, even Shalane knew she should have too after the scene she witnessed—but sadly, neither one of them moved.

BLESSING SLOWLY WALKED to her door, in no hurry to answer it. She knew it was either Shalane or Egypt. They had told her they were coming. At first, she had ignored them but finally agreed because she had prayed on it, trusting God to work it all out for her.

Opening her door, she not only spotted Shalane, who looked like she had been crying, and Egypt, whose expression was unreadable, but she also saw Will. Blessing stood back, allowing all three to step inside.

"Blessing, I am sorry." Shalane was the first to speak.

"I asked you not to tell him," was all she replied.

"She didn't." Will interrupted. "She told me, as she does everything, and I told him."

"Great."

"Either way, Blessing, I am so sorry." Shalane apologized.

Blessing stood there for a second before she spoke.

"It's cool." She dismissed. Blessing didn't hold grudges, and even if she did, Shalane was her best friend, so she couldn't stay mad at her forever.

"You forgive me?' Shalane asked, stepping closer to her.

"I do." Blessing smiled.

Shalane leaned in, hugging her.

"I am so sorry," she whispered in her ear. "Love you."

"Love you too." Blessing smiled.

Shalane stepped back, pulling Will's hand.

"Come on." She pulled him to the second bedroom in Blessing's house. Blessing and Egypt needed to talk alone.

Blessing sat on her couch but never said a word. She didn't have anything to say. Egypt had hurt her, and unlike Shalane, his hurt was deeper.

"Look at me," his deep voice demanded.

Hesitant at first, Blessing slowly lifted her eyes, glaring at him. Instantly, tears fell. She trusted Egypt. She believed in him. She felt protected by him, yet he broke everything in her when he said the things he did.

"I'm sorry." She dropped her head, covering her mouth as

she cried, apologizing for crying—nothing more and nothing less.

He had fucked up, and he knew it. Nothing that he had said earlier was how he felt, but at the moment, it felt like the right words. Seeing her cry now broke him.

Standing, he walked to her, pulling her to her feet. The moment he did, she smacked him. He deserved that. The smack stung his cheek, but that didn't stop him from pulling her closer to him, holding her tightly as she cried.

"Blessing, I'm sorry." He leaned down, kissing her forehead.

Hearing him say sorry caused her to look up into his eyes that were waiting to meet hers. Blessing knew Egypt. She knew his weaknesses. She knew his strengths. Though he seemed strong right now as he held her, she saw fear. She saw pain in his eyes.

"I fucked up, Blessing. I fucked up big time. I hope you believe me when I say I'm sorry. I know who you are, and I know that baby is mine. I let my ego get the best of me, and I fucked up," he repeated.

"Blessing, I love you, and no matter how much I try to ignore that or even pretend that shit ain't there, it is. I'on wanna be without you no more, and that's me being honest."

Blessing had never really heard him talk this way, but she enjoyed hearing him express himself. So many things raced through Blessing's mind as she eyed him. They hadn't said I love you since Halloween night, but it didn't mean she didn't love him. She had been running from him long enough, but why keep running when he was about to be the father of her child? Not only that, but the love she had for him was unbreakable.

"Egypt," she spoke lowly. "I love you so much." She reached up, touching his face, causing him to smile. She didn't see his smile often, but when she did, it lit up a room. "I w—"

Her words were cut off when Egypt kissed her. They missed each other, but when they kissed, it was as if they hadn't been apart for one second.

Egypt pulled back from the kiss, running his fingers through her hair.

"I love you," he told her again as he brushed away the last of her tears.

She smiled wide. "I love you."

They had made amends and would be okay.

Twenty-Three

March 2018

"Yo?" Egypt answered his vibrating cell phone in a groggy tone. "Em, she did what?" He moved his arm from under Blessing so he could sit up in the bed. "Fuck. A'ight, I'm on my way."

He turned the lamp on that was on his nightstand.

"What's wrong?" Blessing asked, sitting up as well.

"Martika put Em out." He slid on his jeans before pulling his shirt on over her head.

"It's two in the morning. Why would she put her child out?" Blessing asked in a confused tone.

"I'on know, but I have to get my daughter."

She scooted from the bed. "I'm coming."

"Baby, you don't have to. It's late, and we have our first prenatal appointment in the morning."

"I said I'm coming, Egypt." She insisted.

Egypt stood from the bed. He wanted to protest, but it was pointless.

"Well, come on, baby, 'cause she is legit outside."

"Wow," Blessing mumbled, quickly getting dressed, wondering how anyone could put their child out, especially at two in the damn morning.

———

"SHE CAN'T STAY HERE! She gotta fucking go!" Marika yelled, and Blessing instantly knew she had been drinking.

"Fuck you put her out for? She just turned sixteen, and you put her out on the street. Who the fuck does that?"

"I do!" she spat. "Her ass always wanna be fucking disrespectful! Got them little, nappy-head ass boys sneaking in and shit! Nah, she can't stay the fuck up in here!" Martika lit a cigarette.

"Why the hell didn't you just call me or have her call me? I could have come and got her before you put her out, Tika."

"This my motherfucking shit! I do what the fuck I want!" was her only reply. "Like I said, she can't stay here."

Egypt pinched the bridge of his nose. He didn't understand how she could justify her actions.

"She's coming with me."

"Yeah, take her ass with you. Let her be in your shit disrespecting you and that chick you laid up, playing house, with."

Martika was clearly jealous, and Egypt couldn't help but laugh. How was she jealous when she had kids younger than their daughter and a dude laid up in her crib on a daily?

"We gone," he said, walking behind Empress, who was already out the door..

"Don't bring her ass back up in here!" she yelled after them.

"Go ahead up," Egypt told Blessing after they'd made it back to his house. "I have to talk to Empress for a min." Egypt kissed Blessing before she took the stairs.

Egypt pinched the bridge of nose as he watched her walked up the stairs, not moving until she was out of sight. He took out a Black from his pocket, sparking it as he walked into the kitchen, where he spotted Empress getting a soda out of his fridge.

"Sit down, Empress. Let me talk to you." His voice was calm as he inhaled the smoke, letting it out before he sat down.

Without a word, Empress sat down while opening her soda. She knew this conversation was coming.

"You had a boy in your mother's house?"

Empress's eyes filled with tears as she nodded her head.

It took a few seconds for Egypt to ask his next question because he wasn't prepared for the answer she may give.

"Are you sexually active?"

"No," she quickly answered.

"Then why was he there?" He pulled on the cigar, lighting the end of it, illuminating more.

"Jabari is my friend. His dad abuses him, so he had snuck out to have a place to live. Daddy, I know it wasn't right to let him come to Mommy's house without permission, but I promise we aren't having sex. He's not even my boyfriend. He's just my friend, and I felt bad for him." Her tears fell.

Empress had a big heart. She was nothing like her mother.

"Yeah, Em, you were wrong, but I get it. You were just trying to help a friend."

"I'm sorry, Daddy." She apologized, hating that she may have disappointed her father since what he thought about her meant the most.

Egypt walked over to his daughter, pulling her into a hug.

He knew that was all she needed right now. She cried into his chest as he held her. Once she got herself together, he kissed her forehead.

"I love you."

"I love you too, Daddy."

"I'm going to bed. Blessing has an appointment in the morning. You good?" He inhaled the smoke from his Black before putting in the ashtray nearby.

"Yes, Daddy."

Egypt began walking away. "Don't be having no boys up in my shit, no matter what they got going on."

He smiled, winking at her.

"I won't, Daddy." Empress giggled.

Egypt took the stairs two at a time to get to bed. He only had four hours to sleep and knew that more than likely those hours would decrease once he got in bed with Blessing because she would want something—and it sure wasn't sleep.

Twenty-Four

March 2018

"There's baby right there." The ultrasound tech gushed as she pointed to the barely-formed baby on the screen.

"Wow," Blessing whispered in awe as she looked at the screen. She actually had a baby growing inside of her.

Egypt smiled but didn't have much to say.

The technician pointed at the monitor. "You see that flicker?" she asked. "That is baby's heart beating."

"Wow," Blessing repeated, unable to say any other word.

Together, they listened to the sound of baby's heartbeat.

"Heartbeat is strong, beating at one hundred thirty-seven beats per minute."

Blessing was overcome with so many emotions, no words would form. She was happy, but more than that, she was scared.

Egypt looked confident, and he seemed relaxed. Once Blessing's eyes connected with his, she was able to relax. It was almost scary how no matter what Blessing was doing or going through, once her eyes landed on his, everything seemed to fade away. Egypt gave her a reassuring smile before kissing her. His smile was something she loved to see.

"I love you," she whispered with a smile.

"I love you too, baby." He kissed her forehead. Their relationship was so flawed but so perfect at the time.

Nothing else mattered.

"WHAT ARE YOU SMILING AT?" Egypt asked, fresh out of the shower and walking into Blessing's room with a towel wrapped around his waist.

Her smiled widened as her dimples deepened.

"We're gonna have a baby," she said as if she was just now realizing for the first time.

Picking up the ultrasound picture, she stared at it. She could tell a baby was forming, but at only eleven weeks pregnant, it didn't look like much.

"Uh, yeah." He teased her as he began to dry off.

"Shut up." She tossed a decorative pillow at him, which he caught. "It's just so surreal. I'm about to have a baby."

"Yeah, well, you better get with it because before you know it, a baby will be right here."

"What if I'm not a good mom?" she mumbled.

"Nah, don't even do that."

"What?" She giggled.

Blessing already knew what Egypt was saying, but he had a child already, so he knew if he could be a good parent or not. Blessing, on the other hand, knew nothing about being a parent.

"Two things..." he said, facing her as he got dressed.

"You're gonna be a dope ass mother 'cause you're already a dope ass individual." He winked at her.

"Two, you have a little while to even start thinking about that, but your motherly instincts will kick in as soon as baby is here."

Blessing heard him, and she wanted to believe him. At the same time, she still worried. She hoped that when the baby came, she would be a "dope ass mother" as he put it.

"Okay," she mumbled, eyeing the sonogram picture.

In a few months, it would be put to the test.

April 2018

"Mmhm, baby," Blessing moaned as she clenched Egypt's locs between her fingers as she drooled. Egypt was devouring her box. She couldn't even control herself.

"Baby. Hm, baby." She struggled getting her words out. "Baby, we're going to be late." She peeked her eyes open just enough to look at the clock on the kitchen wall.

"I'm not stopping until you cum," he spoke, but his movements never slowed.

Eight minutes ago, they were about to walk out the door for work, but when she bent down in the kitchen to get a water from the fridge, her skirt hiked up just a little, turning Egypt on. He had to get a taste before they left.

Blessing had put up a small fight, but it didn't take long before her skirt was pushed over her hips and her panties were pushed aside as Egypt feasted on her sweet center while on the kitchen island.

"Cum for me, baby." He encouraged her, slipping his fingers inside her tightness.

"Oh, Egypt," she moaned as he strategically moved his fingers in and out of her, flicking her bud, all while gently sucking on it.

Her leg began to shake, and her grip on his hair tightened, causing the rubber band to pop. Shortly after, her mouth went dry.

"That's right," Egypt muffled.

The vibrations from his voice sent her over the top. She was cumming and cumming hard. Blessing began to drip, but Egypt was a pro. He was careful not to let any of it go to waste as he lapped her like she was a hot biscuit with home-made gravy.

A short time later, Egypt adjusted his tie. As he watched her sit up, with a smirk, he asked, "You good, baby?"

"You don't play fair." She pouted, getting off the island with his help.

He winked at her just before going to get another rubber band for his hair. "Never said I did."

Blessing followed him because she had to take her panties off. There was no way she would be able to wear them all day at the office and be okay.

"Let's try this again." She giggled as they both headed for the door.

As she passed him, he smacked her on the ass.

"Nah, let's go. I have patients this morning, and you have your board meeting."

She reached the door, looking back at him. She knew that if she suggested it, Egypt would say fuck it all.

Following her outside, he opened her door for her and waited for her to be tucked safely inside before closing it after her. She started her car, immediately hitting the button to let the window down.

"I love you." She smiled at Egypt, tossing her Prada shades on her face.

"I love you too." He leaned into her window to kiss her. "Depending how long this meeting goes today, I'll swing by for lunch."

She placed the car in reverse. "Okay. Have a good day."

"You too, beautiful." He watched her back out as he did every morning before going to his own car.

SOMETHING WASN'T RIGHT. Blessing felt fine, but at the same time, she didn't. It was an unexplainable feeling. Blessing walked out of a patient's room and headed to the bathroom, but before she could get there, a nurse stopped her.

"Blessing, I'm not sure if you know, but you have something on the back of your skirt."

"Oh my gosh."

She quickly ran into the nearest bathroom, checking the back of her skirt. Sure enough, blood was staining her light-coral, high-waisted skirt. Something wasn't right. She was pregnant and shouldn't be bleeding.

She had to get to the doctor, and fast.

AFTER DISCOVERING that she was bleeding, she immediately called Egypt. He was still in his board meeting, but once he got word that Blessing was headed to the hospital, he rushed over. A short time after, Blessing lay on the examining table, waiting for the ultrasound technician and doctor to come in.

"Baby, relax. Everything will be okay," Egypt said in a reassuring tone.

How would it be okay when she was bleeding badly?

"Okay," she barely mumbled.

It felt like forever, but it had only been about two minutes since the ultrasound tech left to get the doctor. Blessing knew then things wouldn't be okay, even if Egypt said they would be.

A few more seconds passed before there was a knock on the door, and the doctor and tech walked in.

"How are you doing, folks?" the doctor asked as she washed her hands.

"Doing alright," Egypt answered. Blessing only gave a weak smile.

"Good to hear," she said, sitting on the chair near Blessing's side. She squirted more jelly on Blessing's stomach. "Let's see what we have here."

While the doctor moved the wand over her stomach, Blessing held her breath, the whole time watching the screen. Unlike the first time she had an ultrasound, Blessing didn't see a thing. The picture was blank.

Looking to the doctor, Blessing saw "the look". She already knew what was coming.

"The baby is gone, isn't it?" Blessing inquired, solemnly.

The doctor looked to Blessing. Her eyes said *I'm sorry* long before her mouth did.

"I am afraid so," she uttered.

Blessing knew it, but hearing it felt like someone had punched her right in the stomach.

"Why?" she wasn't really asking a question.

"Sometimes these things happen, and we never know why."

"But I was almost fourteen weeks along. It was almost time for me to start feeling my baby move." She sounded as though she was crying. There just were no tears.

"We can do some testing to possibly get an answer, but

there is no guarantee we will." Her tone was still as soothing as before.

Blessing's eyes welled with tears, and though some fell, it wasn't the cry that most would have in this moment. Maybe it was shock that didn't allow her tears to flow.

"No, thank you," she mumbled.

There was no need in doing any testing. Her and Egypt's baby was gone, and doing tests wouldn't bring the baby back. She finally averted her eyes to Egypt, and when she did, for the first time since knowing him, she saw defeat.

Their baby was gone, and neither of them could do a thing to change that.

April 2018

Two long, excruciating days had passed since the miscarriage. Nothing had changed, the pain was still fresh, and the tears wouldn't stop.

Blessing often found herself staring at the black and white ultrasound picture of the baby that no longer existed. She knew God didn't make mistakes, but she couldn't help but to question Him. Was it her fault? Could she have prevented this? Did the oral pleasure she received the morning before the miscarriage contribute to it? She wanted to know all those things, but she knew the answers wouldn't come.

"Baby, I have to run pick up these groceries. You need anything before I go?" Egypt stood in the doorway, looking at Blessing as she lay curled up in the bed.

"No." Her answer was flat.

Besides using the bathroom and showering, she hadn't left the bed. Egypt brought her meals that went untouched.

Shalane visited with barely a response. Her parents also called, only to be greeted by her machine.

Egypt stood in the doorway, lingering longer than normal. He wanted to say something, hold her, kiss her, anything. He knew nothing would work, so he backed away, heading out of the house.

Blessing heard the door close, and once it did, she broke down. She was tired of crying. It seemed like every chance she thought she had it together, the tears would flow again.

She wasn't that far along in her pregnancy, but it was her baby, her bloodline, a part of her would have been brought into this world. So, undoubtedly, it hurt.

"Ms. Blessing?" she heard Empress's sweet voice call out.

Empress was the only one who had avoided her for the last two days.

Blessing sat up, tears still flowing. She didn't want to face anyone, but how could she be rude to a child?

"Yes?" She sniffled.

Empress didn't say anything. Instead, she walked to Blessing, sat down beside her, and then hugged her. Blessing didn't know how to react at first. Her body was tense initially, but she soon relaxed as she hugged Empress back.

Although Empress was only sixteen, in this moment, Blessing felt that she was the adult and she, herself, was the child. She appeared to know what Blessing needed and made it clear by being there for her.

Blessing finally pulled back from the hug, her eyes red and wet. When she did, she noticed Empress had been crying.

"I'm sorry." Empress apologized with a smile. "I am so sorry about the baby, Ms. Blessing," she continued.

Blessing gave her a warm smile. She hadn't smiled in two days, and it felt good.

"Thank you."

Empress's lips moved, but nothing came out. She dropped her head, wiping her eyes, and Blessing sat quietly waiting for her to speak.

"I know I'm not your child and that I'm already of age, but Ms. Blessing, I look up to you. You're beautiful, smart, and whether you know it or not, you're very motherly to me. I hope I can grow to be the woman you are when I'm older," she spoke through her tears.

Blessing was already crying, but the tears flowed heavier as she listened to Empress. This girl had really touched a soft spot, something no one had been able to do in the last two days.

Again, Empress paused before touching Blessing's hand.

"Thank you. You're the woman my daddy needs and the mother figure I need around. I love you."

Empress had a mother, so hearing that Empress looked at her as mother figure tugged at Blessing's heart. Hearing her say she loved her was the icing on the cake.

"I love you too, sweetie." Blessing smiled.

"I know my words won't change a thing or even make you better, but I wanted you to know how I felt," she said, standing.

"You can go back to resting now," she added with a smile before walking out of the room.

Empress said her words wouldn't change a thing. Little did she know, it changed a lot. She was a child, a child with an intelligent mind that made a bad situation seem a lot less bad just from her words. Blessing truly appreciated her.

"Hey," Blessing spoke once Egypt walked in the room.

Egypt was shocked to see Blessing up. Surprisingly, she

was up with her hair now brushed in a ponytail rather the disheveled mess he saw before he left.

"You okay?" he asked, concerned.

"With time, I will be." She gave a weak smile. She watched as he took his black fitted hat off and placed it where the rest of his hats lay. "I love you, Egypt."

He walked in her direction, and she stood to greet him. Wrapping his arms around her, he pulled her close, leaning down to kiss her. "I love you too," he declared as their kiss broke.

Blessing looked up at him. As usual, she fell into a trance before resting her head on his chest and relaxing in his arms. He was her everything. With him, she knew that she would be okay in time.

Twenty-Seven

"Oh my gosh!" Blessing squealed in excitement as she looked around their room at Grandhotel Pupp.

Egypt had surprised her with a trip to Karlovy Vary, a town in the Czech Republic. The hotel they were staying at was the same hotel that *Last Holiday* was filmed in.

Egypt set their bags down, walking to Blessing as she looked out at the beautiful view before them. "It's dope, ain't it?"

"Thank you!" She gushed just as he wrapped his arms around her waist from behind holding her tightly.

This was a surprise from Egypt for her birthday. It was the best surprise ever.

"Always." He kissed her neck as she leaned back resting her head on his chest.

Blessing turned around, looking up at him. Even with her

four-inch Tom Ford heels on, Egypt still towered over her. He smiled at her, causing her to blush.

Last year this time, if someone would have told her this is where she and Egypt would be in life, she would have told them they were a damn lie. Staring up at him and gazing into his beautiful eyes, she couldn't imagine her life with anyone else.

"You're so fine." She bit her bottom lip and placed her hands on the back of his head, running her fingers through his freshly twisted locs. "I love you," she added.

"You are too." He licked his lips sexily as his hand roamed over her backside before smacking lightly. It stung a little due to the thin material of her palazzo pants.

"I love you too," he added while palming her ass and leaning in to kiss her full, heart-shaped lips.

They had just gotten to the hotel, but Blessing was ready to break the room in. Blessing had an undying sex appeal, and no matter how many times Blessing had him, she couldn't get enough of him.

"We gotta get dressed. We have reservations." He pulled back from the kiss with a smirk.

"Really?" She pouted. Her kitty had already soaked the seat of her thong. She was horny and wanted her man.

"Sorry, beautiful." He continued to smirk, stroking her cheek.

He wanted Blessing just as much as she wanted him, maybe even more as his dick tried to force itself free behind his gray sweatpants. They had reservations, and as much as he would rather be sliding inside Blessing, having her climb the walls internationally, he didn't want her to miss everything he had planned for her.

"Just a little bit?" She reached her small hand down inside his sweats and boxers, stroking him gracefully as she looked up at him with begging eyes.

With his mouth slightly agape, Egypt had almost fallen into her trap, up until he remembered how much he had paid for their reservations.

"Cut it out."

She chuckled, and he stepped back from her.

"Get dressed." He backed away with the little bit of willpower he had. Blessing was surely his weakness.

Blessing stared at him, just hoping he would change his mind. They had never denied the other of sex, so this was new to her.

"Fine." She pouted, brushing past him and bumping him playfully.

Egypt only chuckled as he watched her walk away.

BLESSING SAT across from Egypt at *Restaurace Le Marché Karlovy Vary*. The restaurant was elegant. Nothing on the menu was below fifty dollars. Blessing appreciated it all, but she was scared to breathe wrong; it may cost too much money.

Egypt had reserved the head chef VIP menu, which included the head chef personally preparing a several-course meal for just their table.

The food was amazing. Blessing had butternut squash soup and an amazing, specially made cucumber and onion salad with grilled tofu, roasted chickpeas, and a chili sauce. And her dessert was a vegan lime and pomegranate cake with a cranberry sauce.

Egypt had sweet and spicy oysters with house salad to start, a top-of-the-line pork loin with a sweet mango sauce, and a side of asparagus. For dessert, he went with the same thing Blessing had chosen.

All in all, it was an amazing experience, one she would

never forget. They had even managed to take pictures with the head chef, who had prepared the delicious meal.

Before everything was said and done, Egypt had surprised Blessing with the staff singing her happy birthday. During the singing, he had slid over a beautiful, diamond tennis bracelet, as if the trip itself wasn't enough. She loved it all.

"Ready to get out of here?" He winked at her.

"Yeah." She smiled, already knowing what he was asking.

Their relationship had more to offer than just sex, but the two of them had mastered the other's body so well that they always craved the other. They had barely made it to the elevator before they were all over each other.

Egypt had a few drinks, and Blessing was drunk off love. First floor, soft kisses. Second floor, deep kissing. Third floor, touching. Fourth floor, Egypt's hand found its way under Blessing's dress and to her wet center, his fingers strumming her pearl lightly. They had barely made it to their fifth-floor room before they were undressed.

After Egypt pulled back the thick comforter, Blessing fell back gracefully onto the luxury sheets. She watched him the entire time. She wanted him so bad that her kitty throbbed. He placed his knee on the bed, pressing her legs open with it.

Reaching up as he positioned himself between her legs, she ran her fingers from his chest to his abs. He was pure perfection. While biting her bottom lip, she spread her legs further, welcoming her man to fill her.

Egypt slowly entered her, one hand firmly pressed on the bed, the other pressed on the wall as his dick guided itself into her. They held each other's gaze before either of them moved. It was legit something out of a movie. Whenever they had sex, it was memorable, even their quickies held meaning. They both left lasting impressions.

"Happy birthday, baby." His voice was low as he slowly stroked her.

A happy birthday it surely was. Egypt had made sure that, along with everything else he did for her, her twenty-fifth birthday would never be forgotten.

Twenty-Eight

June 2018

"**B**aby, I really don't understand why you have to go to get snacks before the movies when they have snacks there." Egypt chuckled, placing Blessing's car in park in front of the store.

"Man, those snacks are expensive as hell. Why spend like six dollars for something you can get for two?" She giggled, getting out of the car.

It had been two months since the miscarriage, and Blessing was a lot better with dealing with it. She even went to therapy with her pastor. Being able to talk about the loss helped tremendously. Egypt also attended a few sessions.

"You act like we broke and can't afford six-dollar snacks." He laughed.

"Grab me some Skittles, and Sour Patch Kids," he called out.

"Yeah, like I thought." She closed the door, giggling.

They were going to the movies to see *Annabelle 3*. This

was their first date in months. Empress had tried to tag along, and though Blessing said she could, Egypt shut that down. He wanted this to be only him and his lady. Besides the trip for her birthday, they hadn't done a thing except work and sit in the house.

Blessing bounced into the store, already knowing what she was going to get, grabbing a handheld basket so her hands wouldn't get full. Strutting around the store, Blessing could feel someone watching her, but each time she looked around, she didn't see anyone, so she kept it moving. Satisfied with everything she grabbed, she headed for the counter. Two people were already in line, so she waited patiently.

When it was her turn, she placed her basket on the counter, not really looking up.

"Shoot, I forgot Egypt's Skittles," she was saying to herself as she looked up at the cashier.

"Vanessa?" Blessing was shocked she worked at the store and even that she remembered her name.

"Hey," she spoke dryly.

The two women had never been friends, but Blessing didn't understand her dry tone.

"Umm, could you hold on for one second? I forgot to get Skittles." Blessing looked behind her to make sure no one else was around before turning on her heels.

"Yeah, get his Skittles, and tell him I'm pregnant."

Blessing stopped in her tracks, slowly turning around. Vanessa stood with her hands on her hips. Sure enough, she had a very-pregnant belly.

Blessing raised her brow.

"It's…" She started but stopped because she wasn't even about to entertain the idea that Vanessa was pregnant by her man—the man that had also impregnated her.

"It's Egypt's," Vanessa said with a smirk.

Blessing found it funny that the few times she saw

Vanessa, she barely said a word, but she was full of them now.

"Okay..."

"I'm only telling you because I heard you say you were getting Skittles for him, and since I haven't spoken to him since I told him about the baby, I guess you could pass the message that I really *am* pregnant. Maybe he'll decide to not abandon his responsibility since he obviously didn't take me serious."

Blessing's body shook as she stared at Vanessa's belly. Had the last few months of her life all been a lie? Of course it was his baby. Shoot, they had unprotected sex, so what would make Vanessa any different?

"Umm..." Blessing swallowed hard.

She didn't know what to say. She couldn't say anything, so instead, she walked out of the store in zombie mode without another word.

"Where's the stuff?" Egypt asked, confused when Blessing got back into the car slamming the door.

"Just drive," was all she could say, refusing to look over at him.

Egypt was confused, but like she said, he put the car in reverse and backed out before putting it in drive, driving away.

"I saw Vanessa," she mumbled, staring straight ahead.

"Who?" Egypt had heard her, but he didn't know why she felt the need to tell him.

"She's pregnant." She looked over at him to see if she would get a reaction out of him.

"Fuck you telling me for?"

"Egypt, it's your baby." Tears fell.

Blessing's tears didn't give her any warning that they were coming.

"The fuck if it is." Egypt swerved, looking over at her.

"You don't believe that shit, do you?"

Blessing didn't answer. She just looked at him, crying.

"Baby, she ain't fucking pregnant by me." He was adamant as his speed increased, still looking over at Blessing.

"I lost my fucking baby, and this bitch is pregnant by you!" Blessing cried.

She had been a fool. She loved a man that didn't even respect her enough to wrap it up with a fling.

"That ain't my fucking baby!" he shouted, running a red light.

"What does she have to lie for?"

"Who the fuck are you going to believe, me or her?"

Once again, he looked over at her, his speed increasing more. Egypt was angry, so angry that he kept averting his eyes from the road much longer than the two seconds allowed.

"I'm yo' fucking dude, not hers!"

He looked from her to the road. When he did, he swerved, trying not to hit an object, but he swerved too hard. Blessing never had a chance to respond, because her car was being flipped and turned, knocking her out instantly.

Twenty-Nine

June 2018

Egypt sat on the barely padded chair in Williamsburg Sentara Hospital's emergency waiting room, his head dropped low. His shoulder-length locs fell effortlessly over his shoulders. He wasn't the praying type, but he prayed to whomever Blessing prayed to on a daily, hoping she would be okay.

One minute, he and Blessing were in her 2016 Tesla Model S, arguing and speeding through the streets of Williamsburg. The next, they were wrong side up in the car. It had flipped twice because he tried avoiding hitting a dog but hit a curb instead. Besides the stitched five-inch cut above his left eye, Egypt didn't even look like he had been in the same car that sent Blessing to the hospital unresponsive.

Each time Egypt heard the double doors opening, he quickly said a prayer before looking up with hopeful eyes, hoping it was anyone telling him that his Blessing was okay. Neither time was it anyone for him. Before now, Egypt knew

Blessing was just that... a blessing to him. But now, sitting there, hoping for good news, he knew for a fact she was heaven sent. He just wanted one more chance to tell her that.

Vanessa wasn't pregnant by him. There was no way it was possible since the pair had never had sex. Egypt wanted to tell Blessing that, but when he saw the tears, he knew she already assumed and couldn't get it out fast enough. Not only that, but he knew if he said they hadn't slept together, Blessing wouldn't believe him.

He and Vanessa were nothing more than friends. Of course she always wanted to seem more important than she was, but it wasn't the case. Blessing had his mind so clouded that Egypt was never interested in her like that.

The vibrating of his iPhone X interrupted his thirtieth prayer of the night. He dug in his pocket to retrieve the device.

"Yo," he answered, his voice calm yet shaky.

"What happened?" Blessing's father George asked loudly through the receiver. He was so loud that Egypt had to pull it from his ear.

Standing to his feet, Egypt walked near the exit to speak privately. He was careful to not go too far in case someone came to give news about Blessing.

"There was a bad accident," he told Blessing's father.

"Where is Blessing? Is she okay? What hospital are y'all at?" George rambled off quickly. In the background, Egypt could hear her mother, Vivian, also asking questions.

Egypt knew how they were feeling. Hell, that was their daughter, and he was feeling the exact same way—scared.

"I'on know, man," Egypt uttered slowly.

Just as he spoke the words, the double doors opened. When he turned around, he noticed it was Dr. Davis, the doctor that he had spoken to earlier.

"The doctor just came out," he mumbled to George, the

fear now evident in his voice. Egypt pulled his phone from his ear while watching the doctor look his way.

His look was one Egypt couldn't read, causing him to anxiously ask, "How is she, Dr. Davis?"

"Blessing is in critical yet stable condition. She has suffered a broken leg, detached retina, a punctured lung and kidney, a few broken toes, and lots of bumps, scrapes, and bruises. For her safety and recovery reasons, I have placed her in her medically induced coma. She will be that way until she is well enough to deal with her injuries."

The phone wasn't to Egypt's ear, but he could hear her mother screaming.

"Give me about twenty minutes, and we'll allow you back before she is transported to ICU."

Egypt could only nod his head. He couldn't even put the phone back to his ear. The doctor said her condition was critical though stable, but how could she survive everything that he said was wrong with her? *Was it even possible?* he thought, dropping back on the chair.

He needed to lay his eyes on her, and fast.

Thirty

June 2018

Death didn't scare Egypt. In fact, it wasn't much that scared him, outside of losing Empress. As he glared down at Blessing's helpless state, his really short list seemed long.

She breathed with the help of a tube, her leg was wrapped in a brace, cuts covered her face, and glass was still embedded in her skin. She didn't look like his Blessing at all.

Egypt stepped closer to her bed, lifting his hand to brush hair that was stuck to her face under the dried blood.

"I'm sorry, baby," he whispered.

He leaned down, kissing her lips. He wished he could rewind time. He needed her laugh, her scream, he would even go back to her fussing at him.

Egypt stood to his full height of six feet, three and half inches tall just staring at her. It wasn't until he noticed a wet spot on her gown that he realized he was crying. Crying? Egypt didn't cry. Last time he cried was when he was eleven years old, and he had vowed then that he would never shed another tear.

Looking at Blessing, though, all that he vowed flew out the window. He cried because he could only hope that she was strong enough to pull through this.

"I love you," he mumbled just as the room door flew open.

Blessing's parents quickly rushed in with Shalane and Will in tow. Egypt quickly washed his hands over his face, drying his eyes, as he looked on at Blessing's parents' reactions to seeing her. It rocked his core. He had to get out of that room, and fast. So after speaking to everyone, that was exactly what he did.

AFTER LEAVING BLESSING'S ROOM, Egypt rushed outside, lighting a Black & Mild before inhaling it quickly and allowing the nicotine to fill his body, slowly bringing his nerves back to normal. He had sat outside for about thirty minutes before walking back into the hospital.

Instead of going to Blessing's room, he found himself in the church's chapel. Egypt sat on the wooden bench, just staring at the cross at the front of the chapel. He wasn't sure what he was doing there, but he felt the need to sit right where he was.

A few people came in, said their prayers, and left. Some came in crying, while others left out crying, but Egypt, he just sat. There was an older gentleman that sat on the same bench. He never seemed to be praying or anything, just sitting there, staring, and occasionally looking over at Egypt.

"Are you okay, son?" Egypt heard.

"Yeah." His voice didn't even sound confident like normal.

"Have you prayed since being in here?" He scooted closer to Egypt.

What the fuck is he doing? Egypt thought.

Egypt hadn't prayed since being in the chapel. He honestly didn't even know what he was doing there, yet he knew he felt the need to sit there.

"I have." He lied.

The older man looked at him strangely, as if he saw right through his lie.

"I haven't," he admitted.

"Son, pray for her. Pray for yourself. Once you talk to God, everything will be okay. He will never leave you." The old man gave a reassuring smile as he stood to his feet.

"You have a good night. Blessing will be just fine." He headed out of the chapel.

Wait, Egypt thought.

He had never even said Blessing's name. Matter of fact, he had never even said it was a woman.

"Aye," Egypt called out, quickly turning around, but no one was there.

"What the?" He started but stopped when two women walked into the chapel. Egypt watched them quickly pray before heading out. He was now alone.

Clearing his throat, he rested his hands on the seat in front of him.

"I'on even know what to say or even how to pray, but God I hope you're listening." He looked around, feeling stupid like he was talking to himself.

"Blessing is special, God. I know you know that because you created her. I'm sure you want her for yourself, but you can't have her. She's mine. She doesn't even realize how much I need her, but I want a chance to tell her that. I may not be who she needs in life, but she is who I need. I can't lose that girl. I love her more than I love myself. I might sound selfish, and right now, I don't care." He chuckled.

"I just want her okay. If I'm not supposed to be with her,

then make it so I'm not, but don't take her from this earth. Please." Egypt exhaled deeply, dropping his head.

"If she's not meant for me, or I ain't meant for her, make it so we can't be together, but please don't take her from this earth." He paused, feeling like he was about to cry, and crying wasn't something he often did. However, tonight, he had cried the most he ever had.

"Just please don't take her." He realized he had repeated the same thing almost twice, but he needed God to hear and understand him.

Lifting his head, Egypt stared back at the cross. It looked to be brighter, and just as he stood, a calm feeling he had never experienced a day in his life took over his body. It was something about that feeling that caused him to smile and nod his head. Whatever the feeling, it felt good.

Thirty-One

Blessing could hear Egypt talking, even heard him sniffle, so she imagined he was crying. She was trying all her might to wake up and tell him that she loved him too. For some reason, she just couldn't wake up.

Not long after hearing Egypt, she heard her parents' and then Shalane's voices. They were all confessing their love and begging her to pull through. She wanted to tell them she heard them, that she was okay, and she was going to make it. She just couldn't.

Blessing felt pain, but it wasn't unbearable. The problem was she wasn't sure why she was in pain, and she couldn't explain what she was feeling.

Soon, the voices became further and further away until she could no longer hear them at all.

"Hey, baby," she heard, causing her to turn around swiftly.

"Egypt?" She was confused.

"Who else were you expecting?" He leaned in to kiss her.

"Um, I don't know." She looked around. The place was familiar; it was her house. "Did something happen?"

"What do you mean?" He rubbed her stomach.

Wait, I'm pregnant? She looked down at her huge stomach, unable to see her own feet.

"I'm pregnant?" She wasn't really asking a question, but of course, Egypt answered her.

"Yeah, for the last eight and half months." He chuckled. "Baby, you good?"

"What about Vanessa?" she asked out loud, recalling that night.

Egypt exhaled deeply. "C'mon, baby. We not back here again, are we? You know I never slept with that girl. We talked about that numerous times. She even told you she was lying about being pregnant and us having sex."

"Wait. Y'all never had sex?"

Again, Egypt exhaled. "Baby, you been taking some meds or something?" he questioned with seriousness.

"No..." she drawled. "Forget I mentioned it."

She didn't understand what was going on.

"Cool." He slowly nodded. "Come on. We have to get to the rehearsal dinner."

"For?" she asked, confused.

Egypt looked at her. "We're getting married tomorrow. Are you sure you're okay?"

Married? Blessing thought, looking down at her left hand that was adorned with a beautiful, sparkling ring.

"Um, yeah. I'm sorry, baby."

Her dimples deepened as she smiled while placing her hand to her head. She watched him look away from her as he moved around the room. He was Egypt, she was Blessing, this was Egypt's house, and everything was normal and like she was used to. At the same time, everything was different. She didn't know what was going on.

Egypt smiled, then winked at her before walking out of the room.

"What is happening?" Blessing mumbled, closing her eyes tightly.

Again, Blessing could hear someone crying, and as much as she wanted to wake up, she couldn't. Nothing was making sense to her, but what she heard next let her know what she had to do.

"Medically, we've done all that we can do for Blessing. At this point, it's up to her to do the work. She needs to fight…"

The voice was unfamiliar to her, but the words were not. She wanted to live, so she was prepared to fight.

Thirty-Two

June 2018

Egypt had spent most of his time by Blessing's side while she lay in a medically induced coma. He would only go home to shower, check on Empress, and sometimes eat before he was right back in the chair beside her bed. He had brought all of his work with him, so though he wasn't physically in the office, he was getting shit done.

The doctors had slowly reduced the medicine that kept her induced, so Blessing could wake up at any time—*if* she woke up at all. They all tried to think positively and didn't want to think of the latter.

Egypt stood near the huge window that looked out into the parking lot, listening in on a conference call. Standing in silence, he felt as though he was being watched. The heavy breathing made it even more so. He snapped around and was met with the biggest surprise of his life—Blessing staring at him.

"Holy fuck!" His phone fell to the porcelain floor, where it instantly shattered.

"Baby?" He was in disbelief.

Because of the tube in her throat, Blessing couldn't talk, but Egypt could tell from the sparkle in her eyes that she was trying to smile. Rushing to her side, he quickly hit the nurse's button. "Baby, I am so sorry," were his first words to her.

Blessing looked up at him. Her eyes looked distant, confused, and even scared. It had quickly lost the sparkle he had just saw.

"Do you know where you are?"

Blessing nodded her head as much as she could.

"Do you know why you're here?"

A few seconds passed before Egypt noticed tears slowly sliding down the sides of Blessing's face. Finally, she slowly shook her head just as a nurse came in.

"She's woke," he said, stating the obvious.

The nurse pressed a button, and a few other nurses and a doctor came in.

"Could you step back please?" she politely asked as they quickly attended to Blessing.

Egypt stepped back as instructed, but he and Blessing's eyes never strayed from each other. He was grateful she was awake and would be okay, but the fact that she didn't remember why she was in the hospital did something to him.

"Are you okay?" Egypt asked, standing near Blessing's head.

Blessing had been awake and alert for a few hours. Her parents and Shalane came by, but now, it was just her and Egypt alone in the room.

Blessing nodded her head. She could talk, but since she had the tube down her throat for so long, it hurt to do so.

"What?" Egypt asked, sensing she had something to say.

She exhaled before slowly speaking.

"The accident... How... How did it happen?" She struggled.

She really doesn't remember. Egypt didn't want to lie to her. He dropped his eyes and cleared his throat before returning his gaze to hers.

"You and I were on the way to the movies. You went inside the store and saw Vanessa."

Blessing's eyes widened as if it was all coming back to her.

"The baby," she mumbled.

"Is... Is it?" She couldn't finish as she pointed toward Egypt, saying it was his without the actual words, as tears fell.

Egypt wasn't sure if she was crying because she was in pain, the realization the accident happened, or the fact of how the accident happened; it may have been all rolled in one.

"Baby, it's not mine." Egypt sounded confident.

Blessing didn't say another word. She could only look at Egypt, searching his eyes for the truth or maybe even the lie —whichever. She kept quiet crying silent tears. She was in pain—physically from the accident but mentally from the thought of Vanessa having her man's baby.

Thirty-Three

June 2018

Egypt wasn't a punk. He would avoid conflict if he could. Sometimes it found him, but other times, it just wasn't preventable. Today, he had something to address, and he didn't care of the outcome.

Blessing was special to him, and if he could help it, he wouldn't lose her, so he was about to right his wrong. The rain was falling hard against his windshield. He had sat in his car for a minute, hoping the rain would let up just a little. When he realized that wasn't happening, he said fuck it. It was now or never.

Hopping out of his 2016 Maserati GranTurismo, he hit the lock button and coolly walked toward the store, attempting to dodge the raindrops that fell fast and hard. Stepping inside the store, he ran his Valentino Garavani sneakers across the rug at the door as he shook a little, releasing his body of the raindrops that managed to get on him.

He casually peered at the registers, looking for a familiar face. They were all foreign. Casually walking through the store, he surveyed each aisle, hoping to find that familiar face. It wasn't until he walked past the sodas did he spot who he was on a mission to find.

He watched her without saying a word. She emptied a box, placing its contents onto the shelves. Soon after, she looked up, looking as though she had been caught red-handed with her hand in the cookie jar.

"Eg-Egypt." She gasped.

It was clear Vanessa wasn't expecting to see Egypt any time soon since he didn't make an appearance the same night she saw Blessing. Maybe she hadn't expected to see him again at all. Either way, her face said it all.

"'Sup, Vanessa?" Egypt nodded, his eyes roaming to her round belly before landed back on her eyes. She looked terrified.

Vanessa was easy on the eyes. At one point, Egypt thought she was a baddie. Of course she didn't come anywhere near Blessing, but she was up to par.

"What are you doing here?" Her voice shook.

Egypt took a step toward her. They still had a great distance between them, but fear caused Vanessa to back up.

"You know why I'm here." Egypt never raised his voice, yet he sounded powerful as his eyes sliced through Vanessa's soul.

"Why you tell my lady that baby is mine when you know you and I never slept together?"

"I'm sorry," she mumbled. Her body now shaking so bad that she almost peed on herself. Vanessa hoped he didn't do anything to harm her for the shit she did.

"You're sorry?" Egypt sneered.

"My lady up in a fucking hospital because of some dumb

shit you pulled, and all you can say is you're sorry?" He raised his voice, and she jumped.

Tears fell, and her heart was beating so fast and loudly it sounded like it was going to beat out of her chest.

"I'm s—"

"Fix this shit!" he roared.

A few people walked over. He was sure not to hurt Vanessa. Though he may have been an intimidating, six-foot-something black man with locs who was stereotyped against, he wouldn't dare put his hands on a woman, under any circumstance.

He scowled at her before walking out of the store as casually as he walked in.

Egypt needed Vanessa to tell the truth because, though Blessing said she believed him, he knew this wouldn't rest until she heard from the one who caused the problem at first.

"I'm fine, Egypt," Blessing mumbled as she hopped over to her sofa.

Blessing had just gotten home from the hospital, and though she had a cast on her leg and bumps, bruises, and scars on her body, she was getting around well and didn't seem like she had a near-death experience at all. Egypt had offered to take her back to his house, but she nicely declined. She honestly didn't even want him there now.

Blessing had time to think of everything between her and Egypt. She loved him, but the two of them being together was more of a problem than not. Losing her baby took her down a dark road, but now that she'd almost lost her life behind Egypt, she wasn't sure if he was someone she still wanted to be with, even if she did love him.

"Baby, I'm just trying to make sure you're good." He helped her prop her leg up on her ottoman.

Blessing sighed as she leaned her head back on her sofa.

"Egypt," she whispered.

She watched his movements cease when she spoke. He turned to look at her, and for the first time, Blessing didn't feel a connection to the man she was supposed to love. Had they lost their touch? Were things over between them? Blessing didn't know. What she did know was that those butterflies that normally overpowered her stomach when she saw Egypt weren't even flapping their wings, not even just a little.

"We should talk." She slowly pushed the hair from her face, leaving her hand on her head as he looked away from him.

"'Sup, baby?" He sat down near her.

I do love him, but what happened to our connection? Blessing thought, biting her bottom lip while twirling her hair.

"I appreciate you for sticking by me through all of this. The accident, even when I lost the baby... I thank you." She paused as she watched his jaw twitch. He was pissed. "I don't want you to think I don't love you in any way, because that's not the case at all, Egypt. I just need some time to figure out life. I'm twenty-five, and for the first time in my life, I don't know whether I am coming or going. I hope you don't have any hard feelings against me. I also hope that you and I can remain friends." *There. I said it.* She glared at him, trying to read his expression, but like many other times, she got nothing.

"Blessing, that baby you lost didn't just belong to you. You don't think that shit hurt me too, knowing you were carrying my seed and the baby died? Well, it did. That shit hurt to the fucking core. That accident, did you forget I was the one driving the car? How you think I feel as your boyfriend, knowing I was driving a car that almost took you out? Besides this fucking little ass cut on my eye, it doesn't even look like I was in the same car as you." He pointed to the scar that was healing quite well. "How you think I feel, baby? That shit hurts like fuck," he admitted. "You been trying to run from this relationship since you met me. The question is why?" He didn't wait for an answer. "You love me just like I love you, yet you holding your shit back. I can't change shit that already happened, but I want you to know this." He paused.

"You losing our baby hurt like something I never want to experience again, and if it was up to me, *our* kid would be here."

"The accident, baby, I wouldn't have driven away from the store that day without finding out what was wrong. I would have handled that shit with Vanessa right then and there, and then you and I would have been cool and still went to the movies that night like we were supposed to."

Blessing sat, listening, trying her best not to cry. It was becoming an impossible task.

"You can try to run all you want, but I refuse to let you. I prayed about this situation, and no, I ain't no Christian, but God gave me the answers I needed. I ain't letting you go, so you might as well stop running."

"You prayed?" Blessing had heard everything he'd said, but the fact that he said he prayed, stood out most.

"Yeah. A few times actually. I prayed you would be okay. I prayed I could get just one more time to tell you I love you. But the prayer I prayed the most, was for God to give me the strength to walk away from you if I wasn't good enough for you—and for you the strength to let me walk away. I received my answer that first night you were in the hospital as I prayed in the chapel. So baby, you want to run, try it, but I ain't letting you go, because love don't run. You belong to me."

He had moved closer to Blessing on the couch. She stared at him intently, as tears cascaded down her face.

Blessing thought she wanted to end things with Egypt, but even now, she was still unsure. It seemed the more she listened to him speak about his love for her, the less she wanted to be done with him.

"We're so different," was all Blessing could whisper.

"Maybe, but so what? What I lack, you possess. You give me meaning, a purpose. Besides Empress, no one has ever given me a will to do anything. Just like my daughter, my heart has a soft spot for you. Letting you slip through the cracks is not an option for me." He leaned in, kissing her soft lips. He hadn't kissed her in forever.

Blessing was tense, but it didn't last long before she relaxed under his touch, allowing him to slip his sweet-tasting tongue into her awaiting mouth. The kiss was passionate and unhurried as their tongues slowly inter-twined with the other, slithering ever so slowly.

"I love you so much." He pulled back, clearing her face of the tears that fell, while gazing into her eyes.

Blessing was in his trance. He was right; love didn't run. No matter how much she tried to pretend she could do without him, it was proven on more than one occasion that she couldn't.

"I love you too." She bit her bottom lip just as those butterflies she thought were dead flapped their wings, tick-ling her from the inside out.

She couldn't run any longer. Egypt smiled with his eyes, leaning down and allowing his lips to slowly brush across hers. They were in love, and no matter how many times she tried to avoid him, she couldn't.

Love didn't run.

July 2018

With each passing day—matter of fact, each passing second—Blessing was getting stronger and healing well from every injury she endured from the accident. Some days did seem better than others, though. She was getting so much better. She had even gone from a cast to a removable brace.

Though Blessing was healing physically, mentally she was still in a not-so-good space. Egypt had assured her that he and Vanessa never had a sexual relationship, and as much as Blessing wanted to believe him, a little piece of her wouldn't allow her to.

Vanessa was visibly pregnant. She knew they had something going on, so why wouldn't they have sex? Egypt oozed sex. His sex appeal was out of this world, so why wouldn't Vanessa try her hand at it?

Daily, Blessing just wondered if Egypt had lied to keep

her sanity. She wouldn't mention it to Egypt, but it was just something she couldn't shake, no matter how hard she tried.

"I am sick of sitting in this house," Blessing mumbled as she lay on Egypt's sofa.

She pulled out her MacBook to scroll her social media as she did way too many times in a day, more than she normally would if she was working. Blessing was between her house and Egypt's house but mostly at Egypt's. Egypt would normally be home with her, only going into the office for a couple hours, but today, he had a big board meeting with really important people that he couldn't skip out on.

Blessing scrolled her timeline, liking and commenting on things she usually didn't have the time for. As she was scrolling, she saw a message indicator on the right-hand side of her screen. It surprised her because she never received messages there.

Reluctantly, she clicked on the icon. She originally didn't see a message. It wasn't until she went to her message requests that she saw she had a message.

Vanessa Shakedowngetemup Jones? Blessing scrunched her nose at the name alone.

"This the most ghetto crap I have ever saw." She chuckled, opening the message.

It didn't register for Blessing who the page belonged to until she started reading the message that was sent to her.

Blessing, I am almost positive you don't even want to hear anything I have to say, and that is fine, but I am doing my part, so you can either accept it or not. That night you came into the store, I told you I was having Egypt's baby. I lied. It is what it is, but know it ain't his baby. You don't even have to write back, 'cause it's pointless. Anyway, you know now.

"This mother f—" Blessing cut her curse word short as she stared at the message.

How did she feel she had the right to have an attitude

when she was the one who had lied? Blessing was so pissed at how poorly the message was written.

She chuckled in disbelief. "That wasn't even an apology."

Blessing had been fooled. She had actually taken the word of an obviously ghetto chick over the man who had been nothing but honest with her.

Deleting the message, Blessing exited out of Facebook. She had been made a fool of. That almost cost her, her life. She sat in shock. This chick had really caused all this trouble and didn't even send a genuine apology. One thing Blessing knew was, though Vanessa may not have apologized correctly, she owed Egypt a correct one.

EGYPT WOULD BE HOME any minute, and Blessing was nervous about facing him. Empress was staying with one of her friends from school tonight, so everything Blessing had planned would work out right.

The sound of the garage lifting caused Blessing's heartbeat to increase.

"Whew. Okay, here it goes." She exhaled deeply just as the door opened, and Egypt stepped in.

His tie was already loosened. He pushed the door closed by leaning against it as he stared at Blessing while she sat on the couch. He could see her down the small hall from the door he entered through.

"Damn," he mumbled.

Besides kissing and a few touches that lingered longer than others, they hadn't had sex in months. As much as Egypt wanted Blessing, he was following her lead, waiting for her to be ready. Today was obviously the day.

Blessing sat, biting her lip. She was nervous, but the way Egypt was already eye-fucking her let her know he was digging the way she was looking. Blessing had straightened her hair, and it was pushed to one side as she stood there without a brace on her leg. She wore a light-purple, sheer negligee that gave view of her perfectly shaped areolas.

Nerves had consumed Blessing's body, causing her to tremble. They slowly faded as Egypt walked to her, and she got a full view of his dick print that had already risen to attention. She had succeeded at turning him on.

"You're fucking beautiful." Egypt stood in front of her as she looked up at him, grabbing the sides of her face, kissing her.

Their lips brushed across the other's slowly and passionately. As he lifted her from her feet, he was careful not to hit her leg as the kiss intensified. Blessing wrapped her legs around his waist. While wrapping his arms around her backside, her hands intertwined around his neck.

They never broke or slowed the kiss as Egypt carried her up the stairs to the bedroom. He stood with her still in his arms as she pulled back, staring deeply in his eyes while unbuttoning his shirt one button at a time.

She needed her man. She needed to feel him inside of her. She would apologize with her words, but she would use sex for now.

She pushed his shirt off his shoulders as he sat on the bed and she straddled him. Once it was at his wrists, he released it, letting the shirt fall. Egypt's body was pure perfection. Blessing was sure God had sculpted him out of heavenly dust, not the regular dirt he used for the rest of the men. No, Egypt was made with godly dirt.

They both slowly undressed each other as they placed kisses in places they knew were a turn-on. Blessing threw her head back in total bliss as Egypt placed kisses on her shoulder while he stood laying her down. He took his pants off before getting on the bed between Blessing's legs, positioning himself on top of her. Blessing tossed her head back again as Egypt wrapped his hands gently around her neck, finding her warmth with his manhood. Slowly, he entered her as nibbled at her ear.

"Ah." Blessing let out a small whimper.

"You okay?" Egypt stopped, looking down at her.

"Yeah. Keep going." She encouraged him.

Blessing had only whimpered because he was piercing her center after not having sex for a while. She had to get reacquainted. Once inside, her tightness suctioned him as if her walls were molded just for him.

"Shit," he uttered in a low whisper as they fell into a smooth pace.

Blessing held his gaze while his hands wrapped around her neck loosely. He made her wetness talk in a language he never had before.

"Baby." Her voice came out hoarse as her walls contracted, suctioning him and begging for more.

"I love you." He watched her bit her bottom lip. Her eyes rolled slightly as her breathing increased.

"I love you too." She spread her legs further, giving him better access.

"Don't stop," she purred, her mouth drying of its salvia quickly, feeling herself about to reach ecstasy.

Most times during sex, they would change positions, but not today—one, because of her leg, and two, Egypt was taking it slowly with her, making sure she felt every inch he had to offer.

"Look at me," he commanded when Blessing tried to close her eyes as her body released its natural juices.

Blessing struggled, but she was able to open her eyes, staring deeply into his. He took her to the highest point. She came hard. She felt good. They felt good. Everything was good.

Egypt leaned in, kissing her full lips, slipping his tongue into her awaiting mouth. Blessing soon felt his warm cum fill her body as his soldiers raced their way through her. Egypt didn't move right away. He waited until his dick turned soft before slipping out of her and rolling onto his back.

Blessing slid over, laying on his chest, as she traced his rippled six-pack with her finger. Egypt leaned in, kissing her forehead. They were where they wanted to be most, basking in each other's love. Sleep soon consumed them both.

Thirty-Six

September 2018

Blessing stood in her bathroom, staring down at the positive pregnancy test. She was back here again. She was supposed to be getting ready for her date. Egypt had planned a special night for the two of them since she was fully healed, besides the few scars that hadn't completely gone away from the cocoa butter she had been using.

This was the first time she had been in her own home alone in a while. Since she had missed her period and started feeling sick, she decided to take a test.

"Oh my gosh," she whispered, staring at it.

She wasn't trying to get pregnant, but she wasn't preventing it either. She and Egypt had unprotected sex on a regular, so it was bound to happen.

Blessing was scared. She had already suffered one miscarriage with no explanation as to why, so she didn't want to get her hopes up, seeing that she was pregnant now.

"Okay, Blessing. Relax," she coached herself. "Relax," she repeated. She had told herself to relax, but she couldn't, no matter how hard she had tried.

Closing her eyes tightly, she exhaled before turning to get in the shower. She had exactly one hour to get ready and meet Egypt at his house. Blessing stood, looking over herself in her floor-to-ceiling mirror. She looked amazing.

She wore her natural hair and had taken out the twists she had done earlier. When she unraveled them, the twist out she chose to rock looked moisturized and healthy. Dark-plum lipstick stained her full, heart-shaped lips, a red, thigh-length dress hugged her curves, looking as though it had been painted on, gold, five-inch Giuseppe Zanotti heels wrapped her beautiful feet, and a lone ankle bracelet decorated her right ankle.

Just as she was walking out of her room, her doorbell chimed.

"Who is that?" she asked herself since she was obviously home alone. She wasn't expecting anyone.

Strutting to her door, she peeked through her peephole, noticing an elderly man dressed in a suit, causing her to scrunch her nose. "Yes?" She opened her door.

"Ms. White?" he was asking, but he sounded confident.

"Yes…"

He handed her a beautiful, mixed bouquet that consisted of sunflowers and roses. There was also a letter attached.

"Courtesy of Mr. Roberts."

Baby, I wanted to make this evening as special as possible since we really haven't spent time together. The driver's name is Leon. I promise he won't kidnap you, LOL! This night will be epic. I promise to make it that way. Put your flowers down, get it in the limousine, and enjoy the ride.

Egypt.

Blessing smiled, reading the note before looking up at Leon, who stood patiently.

"One second." She stepped back inside to put the flowers in water before grabbing her gold clutch purse.

"Ready, madam?" Leon asked once Blessing returned.

"Yes," she answered, smiling and closing her door as she followed him to the pearl-colored Hummer limousine that sat in front of her house.

Leon opened the back door for Blessing, closing it behind her once she was tucked inside. On the seat was one single rose with a note attached.

I love you because when the world may seem dark, your eyes still hold that spark. There will be a few stops before you reach your final destination. Relax, enjoy the ride, and soon, I will be waiting on the outside.

The smile Blessing wore widened as she leaned back.

The ride to her first destination wasn't far. Once Leon opened the door, she stepped out, realizing she was at the place she and Egypt had their first date.

"Thank you," she said to Leon as he helped her out.

Blessing walked inside, instantly being greeted by the hostess that had greeted her the night she met him.

"Ms. White, we have been expecting you. You can follow me."

Blessing smiled, following her. She was sat at the exact table she and Egypt had sat. A folded note sat on an empty plate.

This first time I laid on eyes on you was right here in this restaurant, but the first time you ever pissed me off was also here, LOL. I knew when you stormed out of our blind date, I would never see you again, and I was okay with that. Baby, was I wrong. I didn't know then how much I needed you in my life. I am grateful to call you mine.

You've sat here long enough. Now it's time to move on to the next destination to get you one step closer to me.

Ps. No worries. I now believe in God.

Again, Blessing smiled as she stood to her feet, heading back to the car. Egypt had gone all out for this date.

After a short ride, Blessing stood in the parking lot of Trader Joes as Leon handed her a note.

No need to go inside, but this is the second place I laid eyes on you. You didn't know it, but I had watched you stroll inside. I followed you around the store but not too close, and when I saw you deep in thought, I made my move. The smile you wore when you recited your number touched me to my core. I appreciate you giving me your number because that paved the way for where we are today.

The next destination took a little longer to get to, but Blessing was so hype that she couldn't contain her excitement. Once the door opened, she stepped out on the cobblestone at Yorktown Beach. Blessing couldn't help but chuckle as she thought about now things played out here. A single rose and note sat on the beach.

I'm not going to make you walk on the sand, baby, because I know you hate it. Every time I come here alone, I think about how beautiful and amazing you looked as you peered out into the water. I want you to know something... Just like I carried you from the cobblestone to the rocks that day, I will carry you whenever you're afraid or just don't feel like walking.

Blessing dabbed at the corners of her eyes, not wanting her mascara to run. Egypt had always been her gentle giant, but the way he was expressing himself tonight did things to her soul.

"Ms. White, I do not mean to interrupt, but we must get to out next destination," Leon spoke softly.

"Okay. Yes."

Blessing stood, following him back to the limousine.

Blessing appreciated Egypt doing this for their date. She needed this. It was helping to ease her into a space where she could tell him that they were once again pregnant.

Back in the limo, Leon drove her to an unknown destination. It didn't take too long before Blessing was pulling up in front of Egypt's house. She enjoyed the little scavenger hunt he did, taking her back down memory lane, but she was finally ready to see her man.

With the help of Leon, Blessing got out the limousine and walked the path toward Egypt's front door. A note and a single rose sat on a chair on the outside of the door. Blessing gathered the rose, joining it with the others, and read the note.

You've made it this far without giving up. I was nervous you may have turned back after the first place, LOL. I'm glad you decided not to. Take this glass of wine, follow the light that shines, and meet me in the back. I'll be the one in black.

Blessing giggled at Egypt's attempt to rhyme. It was corny yet cute. Picking up the glass, Blessing headed for the back. For obvious reasons, she didn't drink the wine.

Stepping into the backyard, Blessing heard "No One Comes Close" by Joe playing softly. Egypt appeared wearing a suit that was tailored to his frame. Blessing smiled as she neared him.

"Thank you. This is all so beautiful." She looked around at the streams of white lights that illuminated his backyard.

Egypt smiled, then leaned down to softly kiss her lips.

"You look beautiful," he finally spoke once they separated.

He took everything from her hands and placed them on the small table beside them.

"Thank you. I have something to tell you." She smiled up at him as he rested his hands on her backside.

"Cool. Let me go first." He released her.

"Stand right here," he said, slowly dropping to one knee.

"Oh my God!" She gasped, finally getting what the buildup of the night was for.

Clearing his throat, he looked up at her.

"We don't have a fairy-tale romance. In fact, what you and I have is the complete opposite. A lot of women would have given up on me, and though you tried, you still stuck by me. For that, I will always love you. I could have left you when you first judged me, but it was something about you that I couldn't look past. I could go on and on, but baby, what's understood needs no explanation. I love you so much. Blessing Joy White, will you be my wife?"

Blessing was crying. At first, she was wiping away fallen tears, but after a while, she stopped trying to stop them and let them fall freely.

"Yes, baby," she whispered through her tears.

Egypt dug in the front of his slacks, pulling out a ring that he had tucked nicely.

"Oh my!" Blessing gasped as he slipped the six-and-half-carat ring on her finger. "I love you." He stood to his feet, lifting her from hers and kissing her deeply.

She pulled back from the kiss, looking deeply into his eyes. "I love you."

"Baby, I'm pregnant." She waited for his response.

Instead of words, he kissed her while spinning. Blessing felt like she was in a movie. She and Egypt may not have a fairy-tale love, but she surely felt like she was living a fairy tale tonight.

Thirty-Seven

T he proposal was agreed upon. Egypt knew about the baby, and they were both in a blissful place, so the only thing left to do for the night was make love to each other. They had plans to please the other like they never had before. They had kissed the entire way upstairs, only breaking the kiss to remove the other's clothes.

"Lay down," Blessing demanded.

Egypt was always in charge, but not tonight. Tonight, she was taking control.

With a smile on his face, Egypt plopped his naked body back on the bed, resting his arms behind his head. Blessing stood in front of him. He admired her beauty. Her dark-brown skin glistened under the light from the moon that shined.

Blessing's body was a work of art. She literally could have posed naked for *Playboy*. Blessing bit her bottom lip as she climbed on the bed, straddling Egypt, careful to not let him slip inside of her.

"Promise me one thing." She ran her hands over his chest as she wound against him.

"What's that?" His voice was raspy and sexy as he reached down touching her thighs, but she quickly moved them.

"No matter what I do, you cannot touch me." She smirked at him.

"As long as it ain't no weird shit."

"Promise me." She continued grinding as she reached back, running her hand from the base of his dick up to the head. He filled her hand.

"I promise, baby."

"Good." Blessing winked.

"You want a taste?" She continued grinding on him. She knew Egypt always wanted to lick the box.

"Yeah." He caught himself as he was about to touch her.

Blessing giggled as she climbed up his chest before slowly sitting on his hungry, awaiting mouth.

"Shit." She gasped immediately.

Egypt strategically moved his tongue around Blessing's swollen bud as she twirled against his mouth. Grabbing the plush headboard, Blessing rotated her hips with her face to the ceiling, quietly calling on God.

"Baby, what you doing?" Egypt looked up at her as she sat up from his mouth. He could please her all day.

"No touching." She smirked as she turned her back side to him once again sitting on his face. This time she leaned her body forward, wrapping her full lips around his manhood that stood tall, the veins bulging throughout.

When Blessing first tried giving him oral, she gagged, almost instantly throwing up, but she had finally learned how to take all of his girth in her mouth, pleasing him without missing a beat.

Egypt's toes curled as Blessing sucked and salivated on him like a pro. She had practiced on him before she finally mastered it. Blessing had told him not to touch, but it was becoming an impossible task as he ate her box, causing her to rock her hips faster on his mouth.

"Baby," she mumbled as he was sucking her clit.

Blessing moaned loudly as she felt herself about to come. She stopped abruptly.

"Nah. Not yet." She was breathing less as she faced Egypt, sliding slowing onto his erection. She wasn't ready to cum yet.

Positioning herself so she was on her toes while pressing her hands firmly on his chest, she bounced her ass to a beat that only played in her head.

"Damn," Egypt mumbled, sitting up on his elbows and looking down, watching as Blessing's love tunnel suctioned and swallowed him whole.

Blessing bounced and rocked her hips as she threw her head back, feeling herself about to release.

"Baby," she moaned, loosely grabbing her own hair while she bounced up and down on him.

Egypt was having a hard time keeping his hands to himself, and the way Blessing was riding him was making the task even harder. Taking a chance, he reached up, grabbing both her breasts before flicking her gumdrop-shaped nipples. Blessing was so caught up and feeling good that she hadn't even realized Egypt had broken the only rule she had set.

"I'm about to cum." Her body shuddered as she pressed her hands on his chest, clawing a little, pinching him.

She was cumming so hard that her movements slowed, so Egypt grabbed her and thrust his hips upward, reaching her G-spot as he pounded her hard.

"Ooo… Ahh, baby," she whimpered, her eyes rolling the back of her head.

Her walls tightened as she dripped. It was an amazing feeling.

"Fuck." Egypt's voice was low and sexy as he came not long after her. Both their bodies shook as their loud breathing filled the room.

Sex was so good. Blessing couldn't move, and neither could Egypt. He fell back on the bed, his arms still wrapped around her. He still filled her as he slowly lost all the blood flow that had him at attention. Egypt was still inside Blessing as she rested her head on his chest before sleep soon took over her body.

Egypt wasn't sleeping. He was listening to her breathing, and it was low and even. He chuckled a little, kissing her forehead. He never imagined this was where he and Blessing would be, but it would be a lie if he said he didn't appreciate where they were. She would soon be his wife and the mother of his child.

Life was good.

Thirty-Eight

November 2018

"**D**amn, bitch. You got a strong glow going on." Shalane observed her friend.

Blessing seemed lighter and more refreshed and just had an all-around glow. Shalane couldn't put her finger on it, but something was different.

"It ain't the damn mini white house you have sitting on your finger either." Shalane joked about the beautiful ring Egypt had blessed her with. "This glow is different."

Shalane looked Blessing over, trying to figure out what it was; she got nothing. Egypt and Blessing were hosting a dinner at his house for Shalane and Will. It was an opportunity to share their pregnancy news. They also wanted to ask them to be godparents to their child. It was only right with Shalane being Blessing's best friend and Will being Egypt's.

Besides Blessing's parents and Empress, no one knew about the pregnancy. Afraid of repeating what happened before, they preferred waiting until the second trimester to make an announcement.

"You're crazy." Blessing giggled.

"Nah, I ain't crazy. Something is different. Face glowing, hips wider, and a smile from here to Mexico. Damn, Egypt got your ass gone."

Blessing couldn't help but laugh. Yeah, Egypt had her gone, but everything Shalane mentioned was due to this pregnancy, which she was finding to be blissful.

"Girl, come on."

Blessing brushed her off as she walked away to go with the guys that were sitting in the screened-in porch attached to the back of Egypt's house. Egypt and Will were there smoking Black & Milds while drinking. It was a pretty nice night for it to be November, so they had decided to chill there, getting a nice breeze.

As soon as Egypt spotted Blessing, he put the cigar out. He had been working on quitting, and though the task seemed harder than not, he promised that by the time baby made its entrance, he would be done completely.

"Baby, ain't Bless looking different?" Shalane asked Will, sitting closely to him, unable to leave the subject alone.

Blessing giggled, sitting on Egypt's lap, as he rested his hand on her thigh.

"We might as well tell them now because she not letting up," she whispered in his ear.

"Nah, hell are you whispering for?" Shalane peered at Blessing with a smirk before Will could even answer what she had asked.

"We ain't leaving so y'all asses can do it. Y'all invited us over, so we chillin' for a while." Shalane joked, causing everyone to laugh.

"Shut up." Blessing laughed.

Soon, Egypt tapped her thigh, prompting her to stand. He

then reached behind him. Egypt pulled out two perfectly wrapped boxes that had beautiful bows, which Blessing insisted they needed, tied around them. He handed them both one.

"Hell is this? It's not our birthday. Shit, Christmas came early, huh?" Will joked.

"Y'all have to open them at the same time." Blessing leaned into Egypt with a smile. She was so happy this moment was here.

Shalane looked to Will. "Alright. Come on, babe."

They pulled the bows off, tearing open the shiny, silver paper that wrapped the box, before opening the box.

"Read the cards out loud first," Blessing quickly said, noticing they were gonna skip right past it.

Picking up the card, Shalane read first. "Only the best friends get promoted to fairy godmother. My mommy chose you. Will you accept?" She gasped, getting it. "Bless, you pregnant?" Her mouth dropped. Will read his. "I'm going to make you an offer you can't refuse. Will you be my godfather?" Will chuckled. *The Godfather* was his and Egypt's favorite movie. "Oh my gosh!" Shalane was in awe as she lifted the bracelet from the box that had two charms on it. One that said god mommy, and the other, she learned to be the baby's ultrasound picture.

"Yes." She looked up at Blessing, crying.

Blessing and Shalane had been friends since forever, and Blessing may have seen her friend cry twice. One of those times were mad tears. Shalane stood, hugging her friend tightly.

"Congratulations!" Her voice was muffled as they hugged and swayed.

Will lifted his items. He had a cigar and a bottle of liquor.

"Hell yeah!" He nodded, standing and pulling Egypt into a

manly hug. They had met in college, but they had been like brothers since day one.

"Oh my God! I am so happy!" Shalane squealed. She looked to Will. "Baby, we gonna be godparents. Bitch, that's why your ass glowing!" She turned her attention back to Blessing, having it all make sense now.

Blessing only giggled. She didn't know how hard it was to keep such a secret from her best friend, but she was happy it was over. She and Egypt knew they picked the perfect people.

Thirty-Nine

"**A**hhh…" Blessing rocked as she rested her hands around Egypt's neck. Her head was down, and her body was slightly bent over. She was in labor.

Blessing had a wonderful pregnancy. She never got sick, the baby was active, and she barely gained weight.

Over the past few months, things had changed. Blessing sold her house before moving into Egypt's. Egypt had gotten sole custody of Empress, though she was going off to college in August. Also, Egypt and Blessing had finally set a date; they would marry April 4th, 2020, which happened to be the date of the first time they laid eyes on each other.

Blessing had been working from home when she got real intense cramps. She knew they weren't the mild Braxton Hicks she had experienced on other occasions. Relaxed and all, she called Egypt home from work and then placed a call to her midwife. Now, here she was, having a water birth in her living room.

No one was allowed at the house until after baby was born. They wanted this to be an intimate moment. They offered for Empress to be there since she was the sister, but she declined.

"Breathe, baby." Egypt encouraged her.

He had read the books, even watched the traumatizing videos on how to help her bring their baby into the world safely. Along with a home birth, they opted to not know the sex of the baby, so they were anxiously waiting.

"Hmmm." She squatted, and Egypt followed suit.

The midwife was there, but she stood back. Her job was to deliver the baby. She allowed the parents to labor and experience the experience on their own.

Picking a midwife had been a hard task for the pair, but once they came across Mrs. Patricia, they knew she was the one. Mrs. Patricia was in her sixties and had delivered multiple babies, eight of which were her grandchildren. She was nice, informative, black, and didn't take no shit. She came off as mean, but it was because she was passionate about what she did.

Blessing was already nine centimeters, so it was only a matter of time before it was time to push. "It hurts so bad, baby." Blessing lifted her head, peering into Egypt's eyes with tears in hers.

Egypt wanted nothing more than to take the pain away from Blessing. She hadn't been in labor long, but since it started, she was in pain.

"I can't do this anymore." She sounded out of breath.

"Baby, you can." He was firm. "You've come too far to turn back. Baby is almost here, baby. I'm not giving up, and neither are you."

Blessing stared into his beautiful eyes. She trusted him. He protected her. Most of all, she loved him. Without a word, she slowly nodded her head. She could do this.

She giggled. "I have to poop."

"No you don't." Mrs. Patricia interrupted. She washed her hands at the kitchen sink before putting her gloves on. "Your baby is pushing its way down. It sounds like you're fully dilated. Let's check to be sure. Lay back." She instructed.

Blessing was now on all fours.

"Ouch." Blessing closed her eyes as Egypt rubbed the top of her head. Blessing was having a contraction at the same time Mrs. Patricia was checking her, so it made the pain one thousand times more painful than what it was.

"You're fully dilated, and I can actually feel baby's hair." She smiled. "Let's get you in the pool."

Blessing was relieved to hear she was in the home stretch. With the help of Egypt and Mrs. Patricia, she climbed into the inflatable pool that was filled with warm water that sat in the middle of the living room. The water helped ease the pain a little.

"On your next contraction, bear down like you're trying to poop as hard as you can. We will do a few practice ones. Most first-time moms push for a few hours before baby comes. So don't feel discouraged."

Blessing knew she said that because she didn't want her thinking baby was going to come right out.

Feeling her stomach tighten, Blessing asked, "Push now?"

"If you're feeling one, yes."

Blessing closed her eyes tightly as she held on to Egypt's hand, pushing with everything she had in her. She was mimicking what she had been in birth classes. With no noise, and barely even a face, she continued pushing.

Mrs. Patricia massaged her perineum to help stretch her so she wouldn't tear. "Good. You're doing good. Exhale and jump right back into pushing. You're going amazing." She was shocked at how well Blessing was pushing for this to be her first time. Egypt squatted on the outside of the tub. It wasn't much he could do except encourage her to push and place the wet cloth on her head.

"Come on, baby," he coached. "You can do this."

Blessing opened her eyes briefly. She wanted to give up, but when she saw the hope in his eyes, she knew giving up wasn't an option. Closing her eyes again, she went right back into pushing. The pain was ridiculous. She wasn't sure if she was pooping or if it was the baby like Mrs. Patricia said. Whichever it was, the pressure was intense.

"Keep going. Keep going. I see hair." Mrs. Patricia gushed, smiling over at Egypt.

"Egypt, take a peek," she suggested.

Egypt peered over the water. He wasn't really into seeing his lady's honey pot stretched from hole to hole, but he wouldn't miss seeing his baby brought into this world. A smile mixed with nervousness crossed Egypt's face. It was a beautiful sight, but at the same time, it was scary knowing that she had expanded so much that a human's head could fit through it.

"Ahhh!" Blessing let out a gut-wrenching scream as she reached up for Egypt's hand but got his hair instead. She tugged hard, but Egypt endured the pain because he knew what she was experiencing was far worse than her pulling his locs.

"You two, look down."

They both peered into the water. They could see baby's face.

"Pull your baby up, Egypt." She encouraged.

With no hesitation, Egypt dipped both hands into the water, pulling his and Blessing's baby out of the water. He didn't care that he was wetting up his Girard-Perregaux Vintage watch, that he had forgotten to take off previously. It was a good thing he had on a wife beater.

Seconds later, the loud wailing of a baby filled the room just as Egypt placed their child on Blessing's chest.

"Oh my gosh!" Blessing cried, looking down at her baby for the first time.

She looked at Egypt with tears in her eyes. "Baby we did it."

She wasn't just referring to pushing the baby out, rather bringing a baby in this world after suffering a prior miscarriage.

"We did. You did it, baby." He leaned in, kissing her, before leaning down and kissing the top of their baby's head, not caring that it still was soaked in all of Blessing's bodily fluids.

Mrs. Patricia watched the interaction with a smile on her face. Blessing remembered when they met her and she stated she loved seeing black couples deliver. What she loved most about this moment was they were so consumed with emotions of their baby being born that neither cared if it was a boy or girl.

"Congratulations, you two," she whispered, not wanting to interrupt their moment.

Remembering they weren't alone, Blessing looked to her with tears freely flowing.

"Thank you." She sniffled.

"No need. You did all the work." She gave a warm smile.

Blessing smiled at her before looking down at her baby, kissing the top of its head before turning to Egypt.

"I love you so much," she cried a little harder.

She had wanted to rid herself of Egypt on so many occasions, but she knew now, life without him wouldn't be worth living.

"I love you." He smiled at her while leaning in to kiss her.

"It's a boy," he mumbled as their lips continued touching. He had looked while Blessing was talking to Mrs. Patricia.

Blessing's smiled widened. She wanted a boy, but if their baby was a girl, she would be just as blessed. Them having a healthy baby was all that mattered.

Forty

Blessing was in pure bliss, staring down at her son. They had named him Ezrah Prince Roberts. He had been born June 8, 2019 at 3:47 p.m., weighing almost nine pounds.

Everyone came to visit, and Blessing found it funny they all asked who he looked like. To her, he looked like a baby; he didn't look like anyone.

Ezrah hadn't gotten his color yet, but he had curly, black hair, a button nose, and a dimpled chin. He was perfect. Ezrah was only three days old. Blessing already knew motherhood wasn't easy and that it may get harder; however, she was up for challenge.

"Lil' man, you gotta stop with those duck lips, resembling your mother." Egypt joked as he picked him up from the bassinet.

"Shut up." Blessing giggled.

Egypt was already sexy to her, but each time she looked

on at him holding their son, changing his diaper, or simply taking pictures of him, he became sexier.

Egypt sat shirtless in the rocking chair, Ezrah resting on his chest. They both did a lot of skin-to-skin contact with him.

"What?" Egypt asked, his voice deep, causing Ezrah to stir a little.

"I just love you so much," Blessing said, admiring him.

"I love you too, baby," Egypt spoke before she was done.

"I know, baby, but listen." She smiled.

"Go ahead."

"When I first met you, you weren't the typical church, relaxed dude I was used to, and I judged you firsthand, not realizing you were educated. And not that if you weren't it would be a bad thing, but I was just programmed to want a certain thing. Not knowing your 'rough around the edges', 'don't take crap for no one' persona was exactly what I needed in life. I remember thinking 'dang, he's fine', and when I never saw you smile, I was like 'okay, dude is crazy.'" She giggled.

"Baby, you humbled me, like *really* humbled me." She smiled.

"Looking at you, standing over six feet with locs, you intimidate a lot of people, and though you will protect yours at all costs, you're legit my gentle giant. Like you once told me, you aren't what society portrays you as, and I am genuinely apologizing for judging you before I knew you. Also, thank you for putting me in my place when I needed it." She laughed, thinking of all the times Egypt didn't mind telling her about herself, no matter the situation.

"One more thing," she didn't stop there, "thank you for not letting me go all the times I told you to. And a huge thank you for not letting me settle for that God-awful Carl."

Egypt sat, listening, but when she mentioned Carl, he couldn't help but laugh.

"Hell nah. I wasn't about to let yo' fine ass end up with a cornball ass flunky like him. Dude's pants was tighter than yours." Egypt laughed harder.

"Okay, baby. It's not that funny." Blessing was laughing too, but she didn't want the joke on her.

"I was just sentimental with you, and that's all you got out of it." She sucked her teeth, playfully being mad.

Egypt stood, placing Ezrah back in his bassinet before walking to Blessing, pulling her to her feet, wrapping his arms around her, and resting his hands on her round ass.

"You had a fucked-up moment dealing with that dude, but you were always mine from day one." He leaned in, kissing her.

"There was no way I was about to let you go." He stroked her cheek as she smiled, her dimples sinking into her cheeks.

"You're my destiny, even if you tried to skip out on me a few times. We had to take the road we did to be where we are today. Our love was too strong to let that shit go."

Again, he leaned in, kissing her before she could speak.

"You're my destiny." He gave Blessing that smile she didn't see often, but when she saw it, like many other times, she got weak in his arms.

Yeah, she was his destiny, but he was hers too.

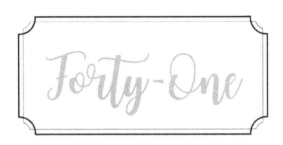

Forty-One

April 2020

"Ezrah, stop running." Empress caught her little brother's hand before he ran out of sight.

Ezrah was only ten months and had learned to walk only two weeks ago. He had been on the move ever since. Ezrah giggled as Empress lifted him in the air, kissing his dimpled cheek.

"Ezrah, listen to Em." Blessing was barely audible as she tried her best not to move while getting her makeup done.

It was finally the day Blessing would become Mrs. Egypt DeSean Roberts.

"It's okay, Ms. Blessing. I have him." Empress giggled as Ezrah tried to squirm from her.

Empress loved her baby brother, as she did her other siblings, but because she wasn't forced to be a second parent to Ezrah, he was little more special to her.

"Okay, bitch!" Shalane put her hands on her hips once she

walked into the area where Blessing was getting her makeup done.

"Oop. My bad, Lil' E." She covered her mouth.

Shalane called Ezrah Lil' E because she swore he looked exactly like Egypt. The only difference was Ezrah had Blessing's dimples, and instead of both his eyes being Egypt's color, he had something called heterochromia iridium, where one eye was the color of Egypt's, and the other was a really light brown.

"You're simply beautiful," Blessing heard, causing her to look away from her makeup artist.

"Mommy." She smiled widely.

Vivian walked to her, pulling her youngest daughter into the tightest hug she had ever given her. Blessing didn't want to let go.

"Today is your day." She kissed Blessing's cheek before pulling back from the hug, looking into her daughter's eyes.

She smiled. "You continue being great."

Blessing batted her lashes fast, trying to prevent tears so she wouldn't ruin her makeup, but looking into her mother's eyes and seeing her mother's tears, she couldn't stop them.

"Mommy," she whined. "I love you."

"I love you too, my child." She took a Kleenex from her clutch purse, dabbing at Blessing's cheeks. "I am so proud of you."

Blessing stared at her mother. She knew her parents were proud of her, but hearing her mother say this on her wedding day made it so much more special.

"I'll see you out there." She winked at her daughter before slowly pulling back, backing out of the room.

"Whew, okay. Let do this." Blessing fanned at her eyes.

"Did I mess it up?" She looked to her makeup artist.

"No. You're beautiful." She complimented.

Blessing smiled, walking to the mirror, looking herself

over. Her natural hair flowed down her back in thick curls. Her makeup was natural yet stunning. She wore an off-white vintage lace, mermaid, illusion-back wedding gown that had a long western sweep train. Off-white Jimmy Choo open-toed sandals rested on her pedicured feet.

There was a light knock on the door before it was pushed open.

Blessing turned to face the door, facing her father. "Hey, Daddy."

"Wow," was all he could muster. He instantly teared up.

"Ready?" he asked, holding out his hand.

"As I'll ever be." Blessing smiled, taking her daddy's hand. Now was the moment.

———

BLESSING STOOD BACK, watching behind the double doors as Empress and Ezrah walked down the aisle, holding hands—well, Ezrah was running. He was the ring bearer.

Shalane winked at Blessing before taking flight down the aisle. She was so happy to stand with her best friend as she had done for her years earlier.

One of Blessing's little cousins was her flower girl and followed soon after. The huge double door closed, and Blessing could hear another one of her cousins yelling in excitement that the bride was coming.

"You look beautiful," Blessing heard her father whisper just as the double doors opened, and they stepped forward.

Jennifer Hudson's "Giving Myself" began to play, and just as *I never been who I wanted to be* was belted, Blessing and her father began the long walk to the altar. The huge church was filled with family and friends, belonging to both the bride and groom. Blessing could see all of them standing and gawking at her. She hated the attention, even on her big day, but she tuned them out and zoomed in on her king.

Egypt stood at the front, wearing an off-white tuxedo with a coral vest under it that rested on top of a white button-up. A single coral rose rested near the breast pocket. His locs were freshly twisted and in his low ponytail. The closer Blessing got, she noticed him doing something she had only saw once, which shocked her then; he was crying. He smiled through his tears as their eyes locked. When that happened, her tears also began to fall.

Blessing stood at the altar, gazing at Egypt as the end of the song played ever so softly.

The music slowly faded, and the pastor spoke, "You may be seated. Let us pray."

Blessing bowed her head but not for long as she felt Egypt staring at her. She slowly lifted her head, blushing when he winked at her before closing his eyes. The butterflies took flight, tickling her stomach.

"We're gathered here today, the 4th day of April, to join Blessing Joy White and Egypt Desean Roberts as one. On this day, who gives this bride, Blessing, to Egypt?" she asked.

"I do," Blessing's father said through sobs. "I love you so much, Blessing," he cried, leaning in and hugging her tightly.

Releasing her, he turned to Egypt as he stepped up.

He smiled before placing Blessing's hands into Egypt's "Take care of her," he said before taking his place beside his wife.

"Step forward." The pastor smiled to Egypt and Blessing. They did as instructed.

"Before the couple exchanges vows, we will have something from Blessing."

Egypt looked confused. They'd had wedding rehearsal yesterday, and this part was nowhere in there.

Blessing smiled, squeezing Egypt's hands before clearing her throat.

When I think about it baby, (Baby)
All I can do is shake my head
'Cause there ain't no explanation, (Baby) no reason,
Oh you must be heaven sent
With your crazy, crazy, crazy, crazy love, (Your crazy love)
Boy you got me so messed up,
So messed up

Blessing began singing acapella, and the tears Egypt had held in started falling again. She was really singing her heart out to him.

"You better sang, Blessing!"

"Come on, girl!"

"Okay, Bless!"

"Sing to your man!"

She heard from different guests in the audience, and though she wanted to giggle, she kept her eyes on her man and sang with love.

Said I'm crying now, but it's not like before
Baby these are tears of joy
They've been the same since you walked through my door
Baby these are tears of joy
Now all I know is your love (Your love)
I tear-up when I think about you, boy
You've got me (So) so emotional
But when I cry now, they're all tears of joy
Look how you got me crying
Every day and every night baby oh

Egypt wasn't the only one crying as Blessing's beautiful

voice filled the church. It wasn't a dry eye there as they all continued listening closely. Blessing always sounded beautiful when she sang. This time, she sang, giving it all she had for her husband-to-be. All of her love was poured into this song as she looked deeply in Egypt's eyes while they both cried.

Baby these are tears of joy (tears of joy)

Blessing sang those last words as the church erupted before she could finish. She had sung to her man and did a damn good job doing it.

I love you so much, Egypt mouthed, wiping his eyes with the back of his hands.

Blessing had his ass full of tears today. She smiled at him.

"Ahhh, Lord. Blessing, just know you didn't just sing that song. You did what the old folks call 'sang' that song. You *sang*, girl," the pastor said as the clapping began again.

This time, the guests stood. Egypt released her hands, clapping, while mouthing he loved her and wasn't afraid to show it.

"Blessing, the way you sang that song, I don't even know if you need to say your vows." She looked to Blessing, causing her to giggle.

"Your vows please."

The church got quiet. A communion cracker could be heard breaking it was so quiet.

Blessing exhaled deeply. It was funny how she had gotten nervous to say her vows, but she had just sung her heart out.

"Egypt..." She began. "Love don't run."

Egypt smiled.

"From day one, I tried to run from you. I examined you with a fine-tooth comb and swore you weren't the one for me. The thing was, I knew you were for me. I was just afraid of falling hard for someone like you. You are caring, nurturing, and protective, and you love the heck out of me." She giggled.

"Egypt, I vow from this day forward to love you more than I day I did before. I vow to never go to bed angry. I vow to always be submissive as long as you lead. I want to grow old with you, have all your babies, and raise them to be just as amazing as you are."

Laughter could be heard in the crowd at her last statement.

"I promise to always be faithful to you. I promise my love for you will never die. I vow to never run again. I love you." Blessing finished with tears in her eyes.

"Egypt." The pastor looked his way.

"You got me crying in front all these people today." He joked.

Again, everyone laughed.

"'He who finds a wife finds a good thing and obtains favor from the Lord.' Baby, I watched as you strutted into King's Arms Tavern restaurant the first night we met. I watched as you adjusted your bag, searching the restaurant. You were calm, relaxed, and owned that restaurant without even realizing me, along with others, watching. I remember hearing a guy say to his friend, 'dang, she's beautiful.' I casually passed their table like, 'yeah, she's mine.' I knew then you were the one. Our road didn't immediately lead us to love, but one thing I knew was I didn't want to live without you. I wake up every day wanting to be a better version of me for you.

"I stand here today, in front of our family and friends, promising that I will always listen when you need an ear. I will always be that shoulder for you to cry on and wipe your tears when needed. Baby, I promise to never go to bed angry. I promise to let you always put your cold feet on me because I know if I don't, you can't fall asleep."

He caused laughter again.

"Seriously though, baby, I promise to always be faithful. To be an amazing dad to our children. Speaking of, thank you for always treating Empress as yours when you didn't have to, so much so that she looks up to you. My love for you will grow each day. I thank you for choosing me out of everyone else you could have chosen. I will always love you, today, tomorrow, and forever. I am blessed to call you mine." He winked at her just as he finished before releasing one of his hands from hers to brush her tears from her cheek.

I love you, he mouthed.

"If there is anyone here who doesn't see fit for Blessing and Egypt to become one, speak now, or forever hold your peace," the pastor said, and when he did Egypt, turned to the crowd, lifting his suit jacket, exposing his 9 mm gun. Everyone laughed.

Once the laughter subsided, no one said a thing, so no one was objecting.

"Egypt." She turned to him with a smile.

Egypt licked his lips, smiling widely. He knew what time it was.

"You may kiss your bride."

Blessing smiled widely, her dimples taking on a dip they never had before. Egypt pulled Blessing to him. She wrapped her hands around his neck just before he dipped her back, holding on tightly, leaning his head in, and bringing his lips to hers.

Whenever they kissed, it was always amazing and special, but today, this kiss was something out of movie, a book. It was a fairy tale.

With each tongue movement, it was an "I love you". Each time their lips connected. it was an "I will never leave you or hurt you". Everything they had said to each other today was expressed through that kiss. It was a good thing her lipstick was no smudge, or else it would have transferred to Egypt's lips.

"Whew, okay." The pastor playfully fanned herself.

They finally broke the kiss, never breaking eye contact. Neither of them could believe how magical that kiss felt.

"In that case, on this day, the 4th of April, year two thousand and twenty, I present to you for the first time ever in history, Mr. and Mrs. Egypt DeSean Roberts!"

The church erupted with cheering, clapping, shouting, and screams. The guests were happy about this union.

Blessing and Egypt turned, facing the crowd as the clapping continued. An aunt of Shalane stepped up, placing the broom she had handmade specially for this day down. They were already holding hands, but their grip tightened as they looked at other before jumping across the broom.

Today was the start of their new life.

Egypt held Blessing tightly around her waist as her arms encircled his neck as they slowly danced to "Lifetime" by Prophet Jones. It was their first dance.

They were at their reception, and though many people were in attendance, none of them mattered as they were gazing in each other's eyes, drunk off love.

"Sing to me." Egypt kissed her full lips.

Blessing bashfully smiled.

"Don't play shy now." He joked.

Egypt had heard Blessing humming on a few occasions, even singing a verse a two, but the way she had sang to him during their ceremony was like something he never heard before.

I never thought I'd fall so deep,
The thought of your love it makes me weak,
You came and turned my life around,

Oh, You broke me down,
Words can't express the way I feel,
Whatever you want just ask I will,
Boy it's our time,
I made up my mind,
And no one else will do

Blessing never dropped her eyes as she sang to her husband.

"You better sang to yo' husband!" Shalane yelled out, and though Blessing and Egypt both heard her, they paid no mind.

A lifetime is all that I need,
I'm ready to settle down and give you all of me,
A lifetime is all that I need,
Don't ever take your love away,
I'll be here always

Blessing serenaded Egypt with the last part of the song, causing him to smile. She had seen his smile more today than he had their entire relationship.

The music to "Lifetime" slowly faded out as Blessing's father walked to Egypt, tapping him on his shoulder. "In My Daughter's Eyes" began playing as Egypt rested Blessing's hands in her father's before he went in search of his own daughter, bringing Empress to the dance floor and dancing with her. Blessing knew nothing about this moment, so of course it was sentimental for her and brought tears to her eyes.

In my daughter's eyes
I am a hero
I am strong and wise

And I know no fear
But the truth is plain to see
She was sent to rescue me
I see who I want to be
In my daughter's eyes

"I love you, Daddy." She kissed his cheek, before resting her head on his shoulder.

She felt like the seven-year-old little girl she remembered being, standing her bare feet on her daddy's shoes in the middle of the kitchen and dancing with him after he would come home from work.

"I love you too." He kissed the top of her head, basking in the moment with his daughter.

Today was already a special for Blessing, but seeing her now-husband dance with his daughter as she danced with her own father made it all more special.

Blessing lifted her head just a little, looking over at Egypt as he looked from Empress to her.

I love you, he mouthed to her.

I love you more, she returned.

It was all so special.

June 2020

Egypt stood back, watching as Blessing ran after Ezrah while he giggled the cutest laugh ever. He squatted with his arms opened wide as Ezrah headed his way. His curly manbun ponytail bounced with each step.

"Dada!" he squealed, still giggling.

Just as he reached Egypt, Egypt scooped him in his arms, turning quickly so Blessing couldn't tickle him as she had been for a while.

Today was Ezrah's first birthday. He had a huge Wild One themed party, which consisted of about twenty kids under four running around Egypt and Blessing's backyard. Ezrah was Blessing's first, so she had gone all out, and Egypt, being who he was, didn't say no to a thing.

There were two bounce houses, a petting area of different animals, face painting, multiple games, a dessert table, and food galore. Blessing knew the party was over the top for a one-year-old, but she didn't care. Ezrah would only turn one once, and she and Egypt could afford it.

"Say 'leave me alone, Mommy'." Egypt did his best imitation of Ezrah's voice as he shielded him from Blessing as he stood to his full height.

"Leb me lone, Mommy!" Ezrah giggled just before yawing.

"Somebody's tired," Blessing said, stating the obvious.

Ezrah shook his head, but he was tired because soon after that, lay his head on Egypt's chest.

"I am going to lay him down."

Ezrah was pretty much sleep before Egypt even got his sentence out. They had achieved their goal—throwing him an epic first birthday that wore him out.

Blessing followed them in the house, watching Egypt carry Ezrah up the stairs to his room. She walked into the living room, kicking her sandals off and laying on the couch, looking up at the ceiling, smiling.

No one had a perfect life, but she honestly felt she did. Yeah, she and Egypt would have the normal married arguments like when he didn't take the trash out or she left the cap off the toothpaste or the heat being set too high things like that, but nothing serious. To her, life *was* perfect.

"What?" She popped her eyes open, after feeling Egypt watching her. She had heard his footsteps descending the stairs.

"My usual." He winked at her as he sat by her feet, sliding back as he rested them in his lap, instantly massaging them.

Blessing smiled because his usual consisted of watching her sleep, watching her shower, and just watching her do he anything. He admired her beauty, and his love for her was ever growing.

"Why are you smiling?" He peered over at her as she had her eyes closed, wearing a slight smile.

"My usual," she tossed back at him without opening her eyes.

Egypt chuckled. Her usual was feeling like this life she had at twenty-six was all a dream. She had husband that was fine, put it down a daily, worshiped the ground she walked on, and two beautiful children. She no long said Empress was just Egypt's. It was her life that she lived daily, yet it was still unbelievable.

"You stuck with me for life." Egypt chuckled.

"Same, baby. Ain't no running now."

"I'on wanna run."

Blessing heard his tone of voice, and the way it sounded caused her to open her eyes, sitting up on her elbows before looking at him.

"Whatchu trying do?"

"Whatever you wanna do, Mrs. Roberts."

Blessing knew what time it was. She felt his manhood grow under the fabric of his jeans, poking at her feet as he continued massaging them. Moving her feet, she got on all fours and crawled to him. She gave him an eyeful of her bare breasts that was once covered by her strapless sundress.

Straddling him, she ran her fingers through his loose locs while grinding on him. The thin material from her panties was doing little to shield her from his rock-hard dick, which sent her over the top.

"I'm trying to do you, baby, for the rest of our lives." She nibbled on his bottom lip as he smacked her ass before palming it.

Reaching down, she unzipped his jeans while pushing her panties to the side before positioning her sweet heat over his dick as she slid down slowly while staring into his eyes. They had sex on so many occasions, but each time, it was more special than the last.

"I love you," she moaned as she began to rock her hips while he held on tightly.

"I love you too, baby." He stared into her eyes, silently thanking God.

She was truly his Blessing.

The End

ALSO BY CHERISH AMORE

Promise

Leap of Love

Behind These Eyes

Learning to Love

ABOUT THE AUTHOR

Author Cherish Amore was born and raised in Williamsburg, Virginia. Ever since an early age, she used words to express her inner emotions as she explored freestyle poetry. It was during that phase of her life that she learned the importance of words, the weight and true power that feelings on paper could portray. What started off as therapeutic and an outlet for her, turned into a passion for the craft of creative writing. Hearing feedback and observing how her words moved people was fuel for her to pursue her passion. Her style of writing is very personal, and she wants the reader to relate to her stories and feel as if she took the words right out of their heart.

At 27, she felt that she had experienced a lot in her life and finally decided that it was time to, yet again, put her emotions on paper. She dug deep into her inner history, her most dark secrets, and bright smiles as she penned her first novel. She states that she hopes her story can help someone who may be going down the same road or merely pondering at the fork. She hopes that her story moves readers in the right direction and maybe inspires someone to pen out their own experiences in life.

To date she has penned, *A Perfect Harmonie 1 & 2*, *Not My Mother's Footsteps*, *When He's Too Good to Be True*, *An Imperfect Love Ruined Perfectly*, *Loving an Undercover*, and *Different Walks of Life Joined as One*, and she also co-wrote *Fighting for Love* and *Sleeping with My Daughter's Man*.

When Cherish Amore isn't writing, she enjoys singing,

reading, shopping, couponing, and spending time with her son, daughter, and husband, making memories.

If you have any questions, Cherish Amore can be reached at:

Email: CherishAmore@hotmail.com

facebook.com/cherish.amore.5
instagram.com/author_cherish_amore

CPSIA information can be obtained
at www.ICGtesting.com
Printed in the USA
LVHW041658061120
670968LV00006B/988

9 798601 751636